Published by Rosarium Publishing
P.O. Box 544
Greenbelt, MD 20768-0544

Printed in Canada

WELCOME!

Lilly Brown is a character that I have been developing for quite some time. She is a bright, curious, energetic young girl from Queens, New York, who lives with her mom and loves reading and writing stories, as well as spending time with her friends. Sometimes Lilly can be outspoken about what's on her mind,which can get her into trouble. In this, her first adventure, her quick wits and ability to express just what she thinks might be the very thing to get her out of a jam. Please read on, and enjoy.

-Micheline Hess

Map
of
Ovenland
Royal
Quarters
Greaseteria
Grease
Falls
Town
Square
Surface
Passages

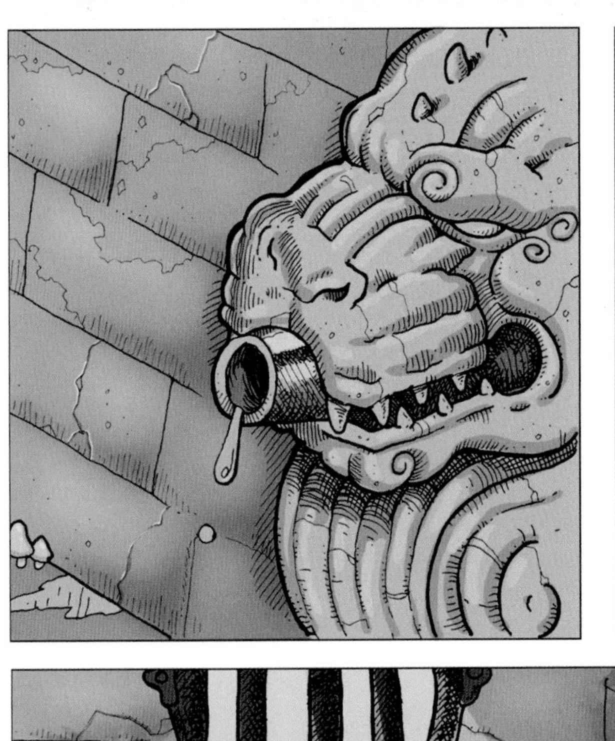

PLISH!
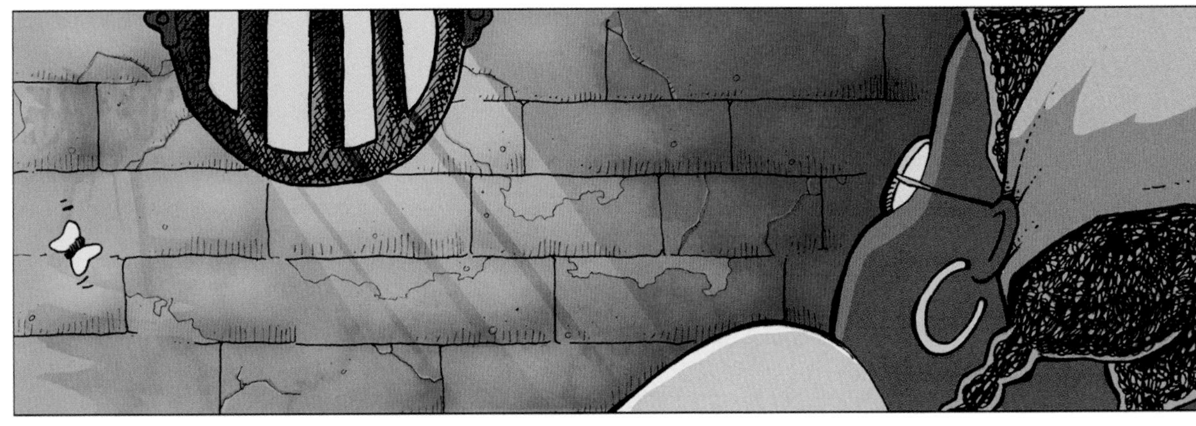

NNG...
ERM...
HUH?
YIKES!
EAT THIS SLOP, PRISONER! I SPAT IN IT JUST FOR YOU. HAW!!!
BONK!
SHOVE!
WHY DID YOU BRING ME HERE? I DIDN'T DO ANYTHING!
YOU DID PLENTY ENOUGH BEFORE YOU EVEN CAME HERE...
SO EAT UP! YOU'RE GONNA NEED ALL YOUR STRENGTH, AND THIS SLOP IS LOADED WITH GLOPPY GOODNESS. SLLURRRPPPP.
HAHA! HA! HA! HA!
EEEEEEWW
SSSLURP!!

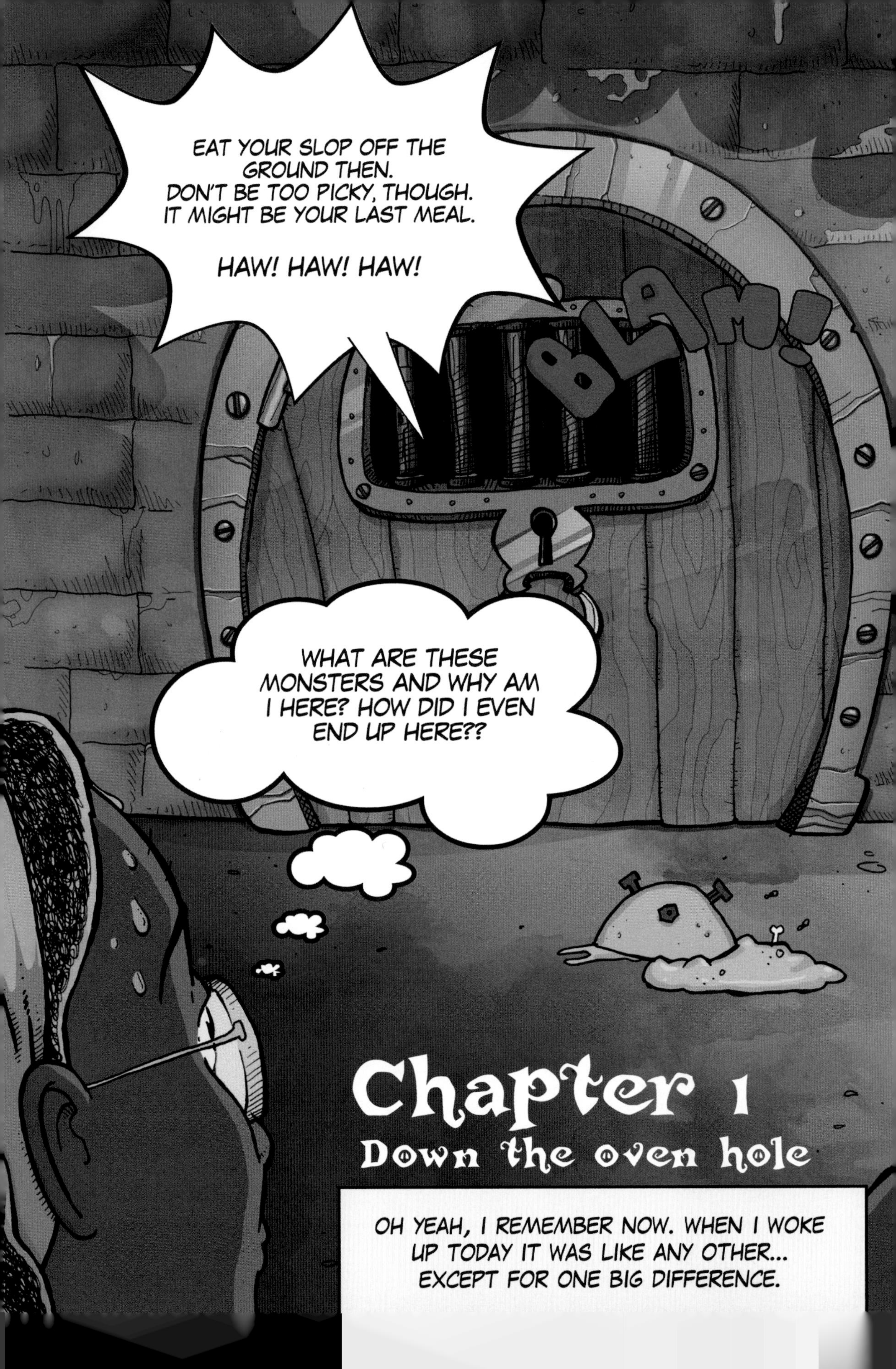

Chapter 1
Down the oven hole

WHIRRRR...
IT SHOULD HAVE BEEN THE HAPPIEST DAY. THE LAST DAY OF SCHOOL.

BUT DID I CARE? WHILE EVERYONE ELSE GOT TO GO SOMEWHERE COOL AND HAVE FUN, I WAS STAYING HOME! MOM SAID IT'S BECAUSE OF MY GRADES. I SAY SHE'D HAVE MONEY TO SEND ME TO CAMP IF SHE WEREN'T SPENDING IT ALL ON THAT ORGANIC FOOD!

ZOMBIE THROWDOWN
JUNE
LILLY GIRL, WAKE UP! YOU CAN'T BE LATE FOR THE LAST DAY OF SCHOOL. I'M OFF TO WORK. LOVE YOU, BYE!
I WAS GOING TO SPEND EVERY DAY STUDYING, CARING FOR MOM'S GARDEN, AND KEEPING THE PLACE CLEAN WHILE SHE WAS AT WORK. SHE EVEN PUT TOGETHER THIS CHEESY LIST OF HEALTHY MEALS SHE WANTED ME TO COOK.

BEEP! BEEP!
IT'S ANOTHER SIZZLING MORNING OUT THERE! THIS WEEKEND PROMISES TO BE PERFECT BEACH WEATHER WI-
7:00 AM

A WHOLE SUMMER WITH NO FRIENDS, EXTRA SCHOOLWORK, AND TRIPS TO MOM'S GARDEN TO WATER HER STUPID VEGETABLES...CAN YOU SAY LAME?
BFFs !!!

LATER THAT MORNING.
OMG, LI, WE MADE IT TO THE LAST DAY OF SCHOOL! I CAN'T WAIT TO LEAVE FOR VACATION!
LEAVE?
DID YOU FORGET? I'M GOING TO MY AUNT AND UNCLE'S HOUSE IN COLORADO.

I'M GONNA SPEND THE WHOLE TIME RIDING HORSES AND SWIMMING!
WOW, DON'T FORGET TO EMAIL ME.

FEDECO
CLACK!
STUPIDY STINKY JOSIE! SHE GETS TO PLAY ALL SUMMER, AND I'M STUCK HERE!

HM? MOM LEFT A NOTE FOR ME...

Lilly- I need to stay at Auntie Jean's this weekend to help out with the new baby. Have these chores done by the time I get back on Sunday...
OR ELSE!!!!
Love, Mom
P.S. Your turn to cook dinner this Sun. LOL!!!
AW MAN, THIS STINKS!!

PSHHH!!
EARLY THE NEXT MORNING I GOT STRAIGHT TO WORK.

HUFF! UGH, THIS HEAT IS NUTS!

THE SPRINKLER SYSTEM WAS BUSTED AT THE STUPID GARDEN SO I HAD TO LUG 2 GALLON JUGS FILLED WITH WATER ALONG WITH ME.

MADE IT, FINALLY!
WELCOME!!

IT'S NOT FAIR!
I WISH I WAS GETTING TO GO SOMEWHERE COOL THIS SUMMER.

ANYWHERE!

MOM'S DOCTOR TOLD HER THAT SHE NEEDED TO START EATING HEALTHIER FOODS. SINCE THEN, IT'S BEEN A STEADY DIET OF MUSH FROM THE OPEN MARKET AND HER GARDEN...I HATED THAT GARDEN! IT WAS ALL SHE EVER TALKED ABOUT.
OH, GROSS! IT SHOULD BE ILLEGAL TO SERVE THIS TO KIDS!
MORE EGGPLANT PUREE? IT'S GOOD FOR YOU.

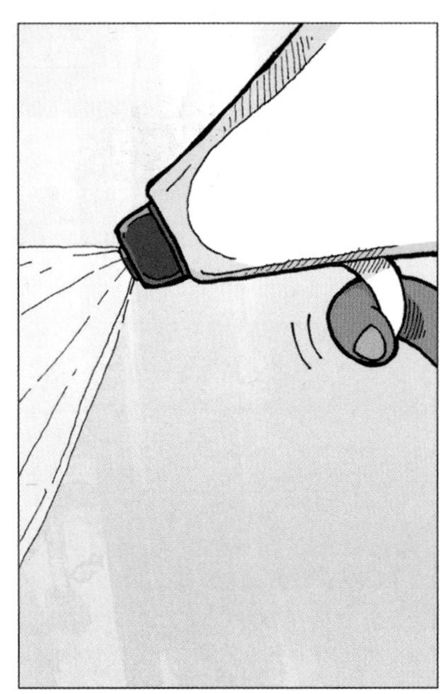

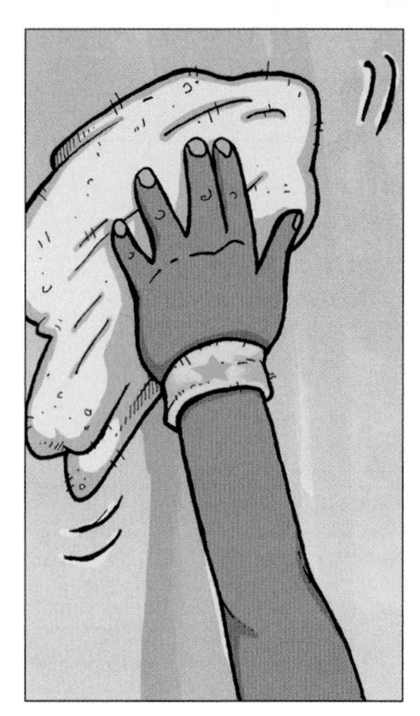

I'M GETTING HUNGRY. GUESS I COULD TRY ONE OF MOM'S NEW RECIPES.

CHIPS
STEEL WOOL!
PWIP!
BUT BOY, DO I MISS THOSE MEALS SHE USED TO BRING HOME! HAMBURGERS, CHICKEN, AND RIBS, OH MY!!!

THERE!
ALMOST DONE. ONLY ONE THING LEFT TO TAKE CARE OF BEFORE I CAN SCRAP THIS STUPID CHORES LIST.

STEEL WOOL HOLSTER™
Lara Craft® OUTFIT!
THE STOVE
YUP, THAT'S WHERE I BLEW IT.

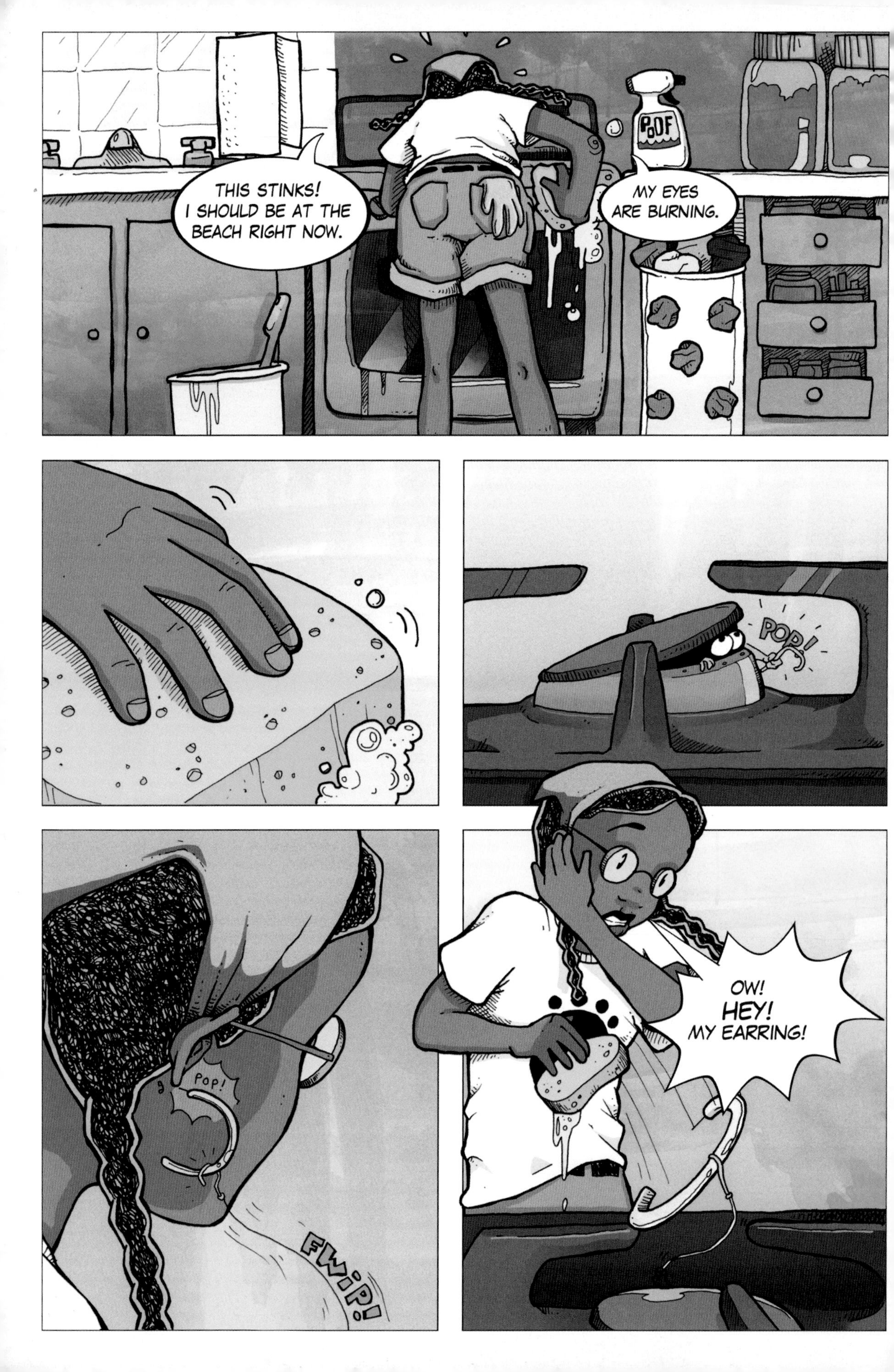
THIS STINKS! I SHOULD BE AT THE BEACH RIGHT NOW.
MY EYES ARE BURNING.
POOF
POP!
POP!
FWIP!
OW! HEY! MY EARRING!

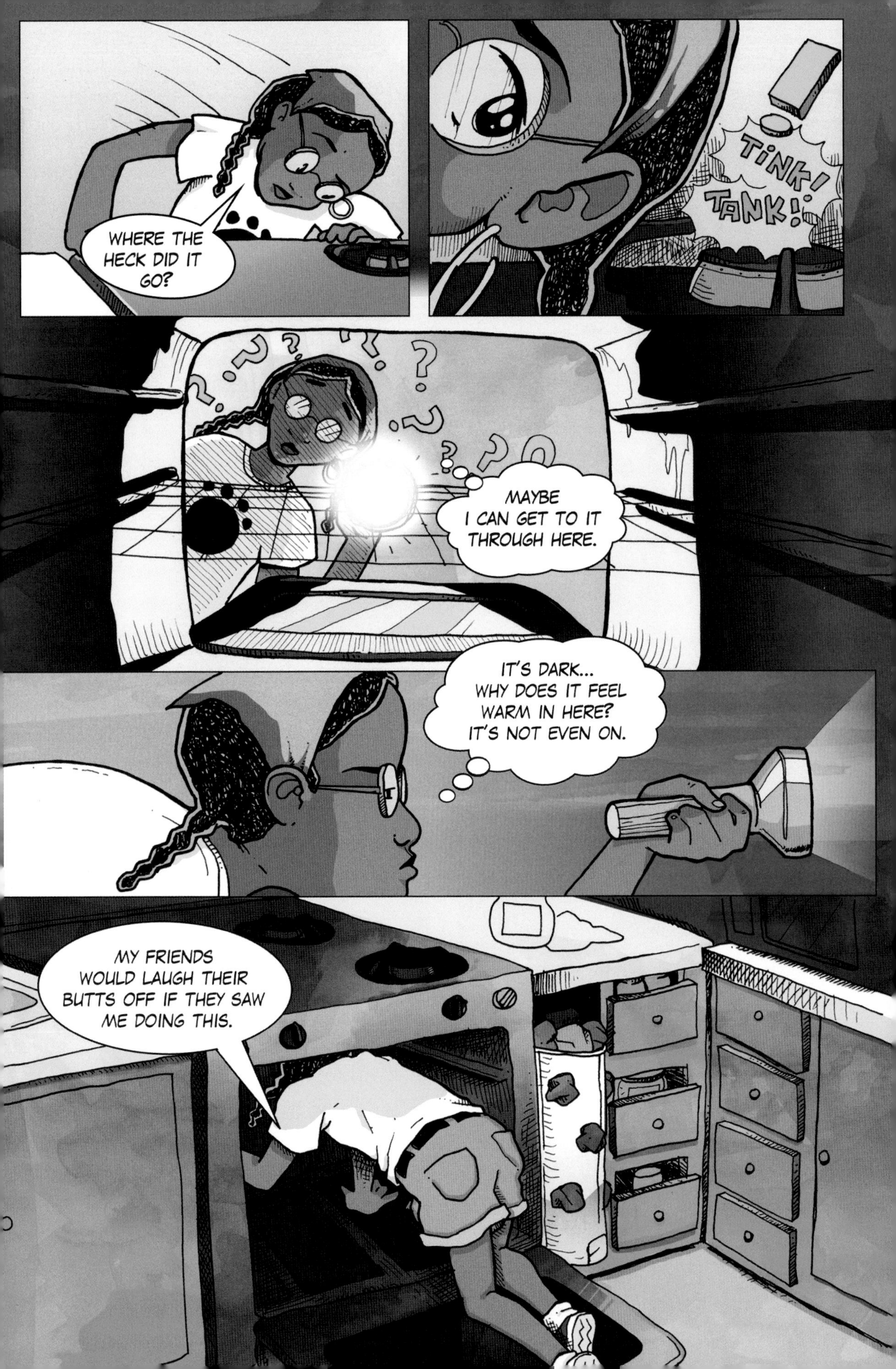
WHERE THE HECK DID IT GO?
TINK!
TANK!
MAYBE I CAN GET TO IT THROUGH HERE.
IT'S DARK... WHY DOES IT FEEL WARM IN HERE? IT'S NOT EVEN ON.
MY FRIENDS WOULD LAUGH THEIR BUTTS OFF IF THEY SAW ME DOING THIS.

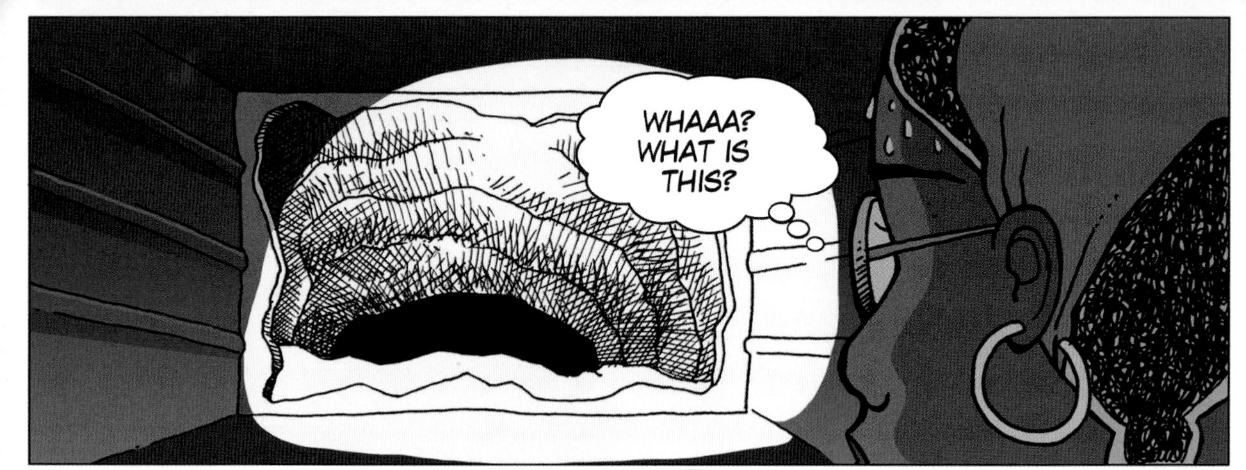
WHAAA? WHAT IS THIS?

WHERE DID THIS COME FROM? IT LOOKS LIKE SOME KIND OF TUNNEL.

IT SEEMS TO GO ON FOREVER.

GLURP!!!

WHAT IS THIS STUFF? IT SMELLS LIKE...
SNIFF?
SNIFF?

BLEH!

SLAM!!
OH! IS SOMEONE BACK THERE?
WWSSH
WHERE IS THAT WIND COMING FROM?
WHOOOSH!
MY GLASSES!
I'M FALLING!
WHAT'S HAPPENING?!
HELP!!!
...AND I HAVE TO PEE!
EEEEEEEK!
I TUMBLED DOWN AND DOWN...SLIDING ON A RIVER OF SLIMY GOO...DEEP INTO THE DARK, SWELTERING RECESSES OF...THE OVEN??

SPLOOSH!
BLECH! THIS STUFF SMELLS HORRIBLE!
HEY! MY GLASSES!
AH.. THAT'S BETTER.
NOW I CAN-
WUH OH!
YOU! STAY WHERE YOU ARE!!!
QUICK! TIE HER UP!
AND THAT'S HOW I ENDED UP LOCKED IN SOME KIND OF DUNGEON FAR DOWN INSIDE MOM'S OVEN, COVERED IN WHAT SMELLED AND FELT LIKE 200-YEAR OLD PORK SKIN GREASE WITHOUT THE FIRST IDEA AS TO HOW I WAS GOING TO GET OUT.
WELL...I DID SAY I WANTED TO GO SOMEWHERE THIS SUMMER.

THIS IS HORRIBLE! WHAT'S GOING TO HAPPEN TO ME?

HO-DE-HUM. ALWAYS LIGHTING FIRES FOR CRUMB.

HUH? CRUMB HEARS CRYING.

H-HELLO?

AHA!!!

CAUGHT YOU AT IT AGAIN, YA LITTLE RUNT!!
HURK--
HHSSSSS

WHAT HAVE I TOLD YOU ABOUT MESSING WITH MY PRISONERS, CRUMB?
CRUMB MUST NEVER TALK TO PRISONERS...EVER! UNLESS HE WANTS TO BECOME ONE TOO.
RANK BREATH
RIGHT! NOW GET OUT OF HERE!!!
RAAAAA!
NOW, TO CHECK ON THE OTHER RUNT... HEH HEH.
I'M SO HUNGRY.
AND I STILL HAVE TO PEE!
CLICK!
CLICK!
CLACK!
CREEEEEE
WELL, WELL, WELL. I SEE YOU HAVEN'T FINISHED YOUR GOURMET MEAL...SNORT!

SO...STOPPED WITH THE BOO-HOOING HAVE WE?
HYUK! HYUK!
I CAN'T WAIT TO SEE WHAT THE QUEEN IS GONNA DO TO YOU!
WHAT AM I DOING HERE? I'M TIRED, HOT, AND I WANT TO GO HOME!
YOU'RE NOT GOING ANYWHERE EXCEPT TO SEE HER MAJESTY. NOW GET GOING... OR ELSE.
OUCH! OK! OK! I'M GOING!
ARE THOSE FRENCH FRY FORKS?
THESE MONSTERS HAVE A QUEEN? IF SHE'S ANYTHING LIKE THESE GUYS I'M GONNA GET IT FOR SURE! I WISH I WAS HOME WITH MOM.

?!

I CAN'T SEE!
EW!
WHAT IS THAT?

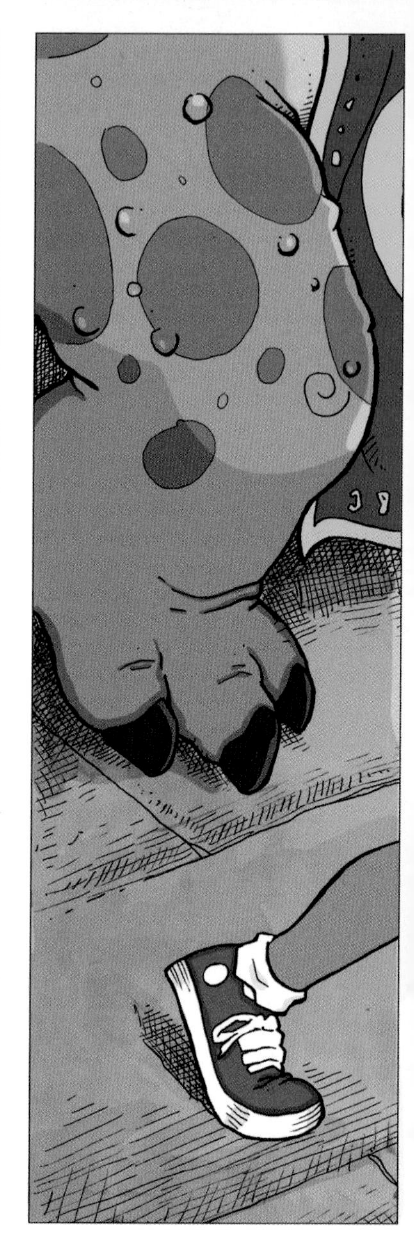

STOP RIGHT HERE! (WHEEZE) WE NEED TO MAKE SURE... WE DON'T SHOW UP TOO EARLY... YEAH, THAT'S IT.
OOF! THANK GOODNESS.

GASP!

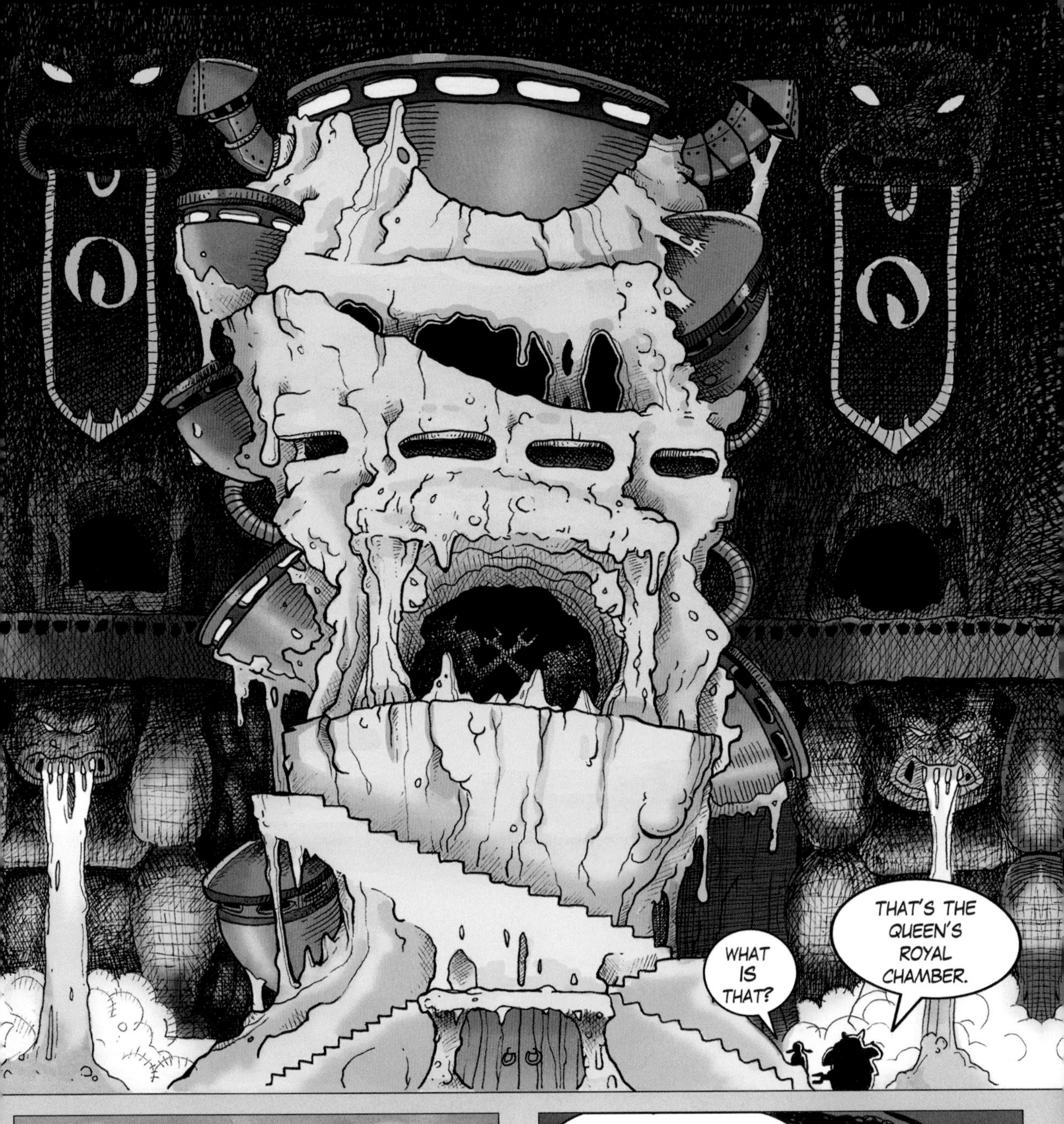
WHAT IS THAT?
THAT'S THE QUEEN'S ROYAL CHAMBER.

UNBELIEVABLE! HAS THIS WORLD BEEN INSIDE THE OVEN THIS WHOLE TIME?

UGH...SO HOT! I'M SWEATING LIKE A PIG AND THIS GREASE EVERYWHERE... NOW I KNOW HOW A FRENCH FRY FEELS!

HUFF...OK...MY CARDIO...
IS OFFICALLY DONE...
FOR TODAY.
...SO HOT.
STOP RIGHT THERE, GIRL!
DO THEY EVEN HAVE GIRLS HERE?
OPEN THE GATE!

STEP FORWARD.
GET MOVING, PRISONER SCUM!
OW! HEY! CUT IT OUT!
JAB!
CUT THIS OUT! NOW GET MOVING!
GAAAA!
ZASH!!

GROAN...

WHAT THE?!

SO...
I FINALLY HAVE YOU.

The Day the Grease Stopped Flowing

Once we were a happy group
We dined on cracklins by the scoop
But then it all just went to poop
The day the grease stopped flowin'!

We gorged on strips of fried bird skin
And sang of grease and all dove in
To pools of lard with all our kin
But little were we knowin'

That one sad day the road would bend
Our mighty realm would meet its end
And hunger'd drive friend against friend
The day the grease stopped flowin'!

But still we strive to persevere
Despite the doom that yet hangs near
Our future is so darned unclear
How dim our hope is growin'

Yet worry not! There's still a fight
To wage before we fade to night
We'll find and slay our source of plight
And there'll be grease a-flowin'!

Chapter 2
Lilly meets the mad Queen
ULP!
WELL, WELL, WELL, IF IT ISN'T THE LITTLE TROUBLEMAKER! I'VE HAD MY EYES ON YOU FOR SOME TIME GIRL... STEP FORWARD.

HMMM...QUITE A PUNY THING, AREN'T YOU?
I KNEW WE'D GET YOU DOWN HERE WITH US EVENTUALLY. WELCOME TO THE KINGDOM OF THE OVEN FRITES. WHAT IS YOUR NAME?
IS THAT AN OLD CHICKEN NUGGET? UGH, IT SMELLS AWFUL!
L-LILLY, MA'AM.

WELL, LILLY MA'AM, I AM ADDIEPOSARIA, THE QUEEN OF THE OVEN FRITES. I RULE EVERYONE AND EVERYTHING DOWN HERE.
CALL ME "YOUR MAJESTY". I WON'T TAKE OFFENSE AT YOUR IGNORANCE SINCE YOU'VE OBVIOUSLY NEVER BEEN IN THE PRESENCE OF ROYALTY.
WE HAVE KNOWN OF YOUR KIND FOR SOME TIME BUT ONLY RECENTLY FELT PRESSED TO TAKE SERIOUS ACTION IN LIGHT OF YOUR TRIBE'S HOSTILE BEHAVIOR.
THIS IS CRISPODEMUS. HE IS MY MOST TRUSTED ROYAL ADVISOR. I RELY ON HIM TREMENDOUSLY. HE'S NOT HAPPY TO SEE YOU EITHER IN CASE YOU WERE WONDERING.
HMPH!

Now then...tell us what you are doing here.
Are you trying to starve us out, Outlander? What have we, the mighty Oven Frites, done to deserve this grease drought?
Done? B-but I didn't even know creatures like you existed.
But you MUST know of us! My Royal Rangers have often spotted you and a larger Outlander on their many excursions into the Overlands.
R-Royal Rangers?
Hmm...
Clearly she is trying to feign ignorance, my Queen. She knows MUCH more than she is letting on.

GO. LOOK THERE. BEHOLD THE ROYAL TAPESTRY THAT DESCRIBES OUR NOBLE ORIGINS.
WE'LL SEE ABOUT THAT.
HUH? WHAT TAP–
–ES
–TRY?

BEHOLD! AND THE GREAT OVEN ABOVE SHOWERED OUR LAND WITH THE LIFE-GIVING GOOP. IT TRICKLED DOWN THROUGH PIPELINES AND HOLES. IT SOAKED INTO THE GROUND AND SATURATED THE WALLS. THIS WAS TO BE THE PLACE THAT NOURISHED THE FIRST OF OUR KIND.
HOLY CRUD!

GREAT POOLS WERE FORMED WHERE THE SEEDS OF THE FIRST OVEN FRITES WERE FORMED AND FED. SLOWLY, OVER TIME WE GREW AND CHANGED. FIRST WE GREW LEGS, THEN ARMS. OUR BLIND EYES SOON KNEW SIGHT. OUR TASTES BECAME REFINED, AND WE CAME TO KNOW GREASY GOODNESS IN ITS MANY FORMS.

WE LOUNGED IN THE GREASE POOLS, BUILT OUR HOMES OVER THE POCKETS OF HEAT THAT EMANATED FROM THE GREAT STOVE ABOVE, AND HOT GREASE FLOWED IN RIVERS PAST OUR LANDS.
GREASE DIGEST
AND THEN ONE DAY, IT ALL JUST STOPPED!
STOPPED?!

STOPPED! WITH EVERY PASSING DAY OUR POOLS GREW SMALLER, OUR RIVERS RAN DRIER, OUR FOUNTAINS RAN SLOWER. IT WAS AS IF WE HAD BEEN FORGOTTEN. OUR PEOPLE SAW THIS HAPPENING AND WONDERED...WHAT DID THE FUTURE HOLD FOR THEM?

THE ONLY THING THAT WAS KEEPING US GOING WERE OUR RESERVOIRS OF GREASE. OTHER THAN THAT, NO NEW GREASE OR GREASY FOOD FOR THAT MATTER!.

No fried greasy bacon bits!

No crispy, greasy chicken skin!

No bits of moldy egg yolk and toast fried in pork fat!

Urp... but d-don't you guys ever eat anything healthy? No veggies or fruit or anything... not fried in fat?
Ugh...Not sure what's worse. Her descriptions, that old nugget she's chewing on, or the smell of stale bacon fat...or is it chicken fat?

SILENCE! You dare to question OUR ways? Don't you think we tried that path already?
Urp! So queasy...

We don't speak of those times...sniff!

Our one foray into healthy food only led to tragedy in the end.

Anyway, no more wasting time! Why have you come here? To spy on us, no doubt...SPEAK!
Urp... Well I...

YOU HEARD HER MAJESTY.
SPEAK! WHY ARE YOU HERE?

YEAH, WHY'D YA COME HERE?

GLLRRPTH?!

OH NO!
I'M GONNA...

BUEARK!

!!!

NOM!
NOM!
NOM!
OH, GROSS!

BOP!
ENOUGH!!!

VILE CREATURE! YOU DARE TO FEED ONE OF THE ROYAL GUARD ROACHES USING OUR TIME-HONORED METHOD? GUARDS! REMOVE HER FROM MY SIGHT!
B-BUT I...

LOCK HER IN THE HAUNTED DUNGEON. A FEW MOMENTS IN THERE AND SHE'LL BE BEGGING TO TALK.

HAUNTED WHAT?! NO!!! IT'S NOT MY FAULT I ENDED UP HERE! IT WAS AN ACCIDENT!

I DIDN'T EVEN KNOW ABOUT YOU GUYS! WAIT!!! I WAS JUST TRYING TO GET MY EARRING BACK! I WANNA GO HOME!!

...

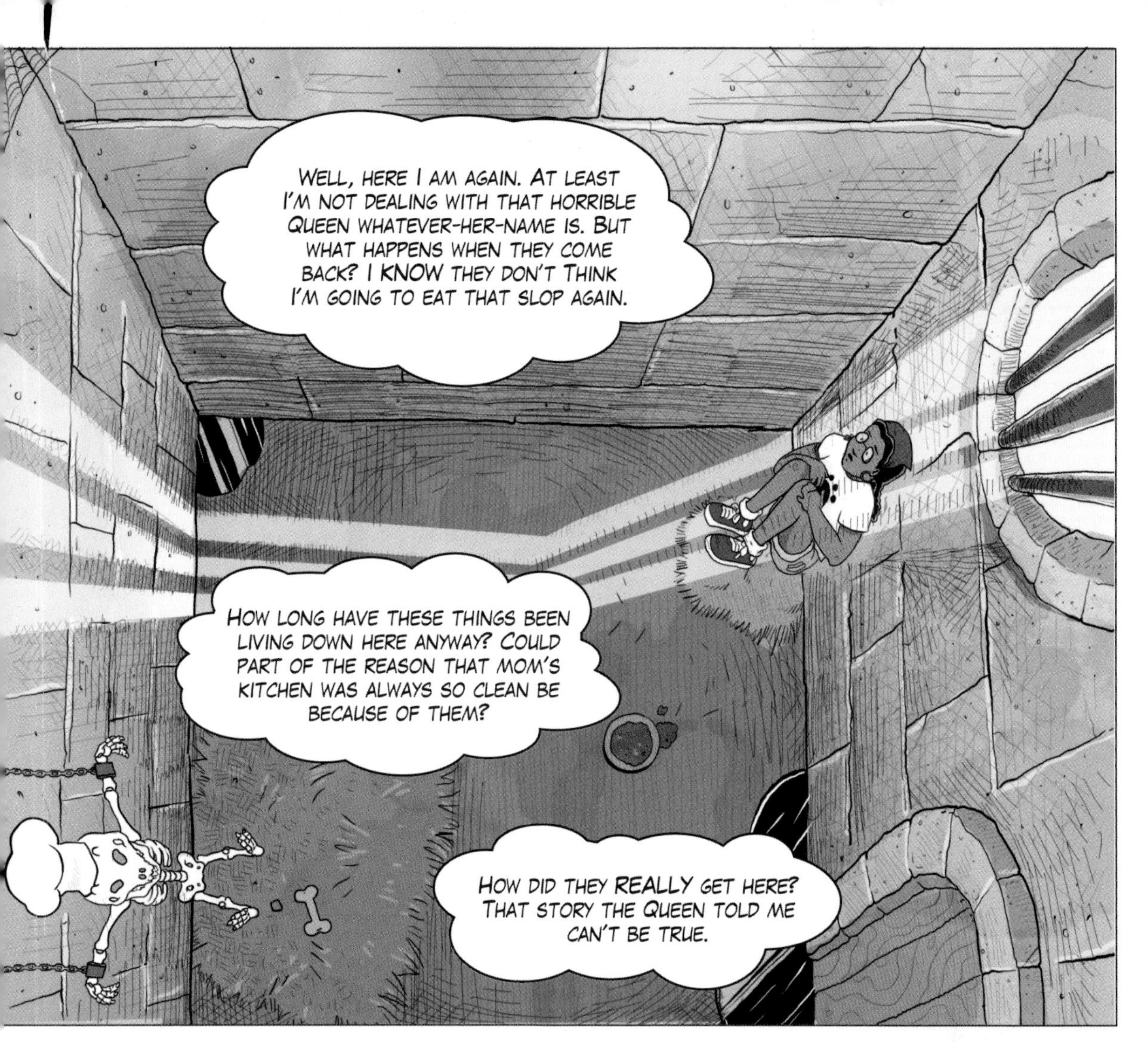
WELL, HERE I AM AGAIN. AT LEAST I'M NOT DEALING WITH THAT HORRIBLE QUEEN WHATEVER-HER-NAME IS. BUT WHAT HAPPENS WHEN THEY COME BACK? I KNOW THEY DON'T THINK I'M GOING TO EAT THAT SLOP AGAIN.
HOW LONG HAVE THESE THINGS BEEN LIVING DOWN HERE ANYWAY? COULD PART OF THE REASON THAT MOM'S KITCHEN WAS ALWAYS SO CLEAN BE BECAUSE OF THEM?
HOW DID THEY REALLY GET HERE? THAT STORY THE QUEEN TOLD ME CAN'T BE TRUE.

HE DOESN'T KNOW EITHER, I GUESS. HOW HORRIBLE. WAS HE A COOK OR SOMETHING?

WHAT IF I END UP JUST LIKE HIM!?

H-HELLO?
HUH?

WHO'S THERE?
IT'S CRUMB. CRUMB CAME TO SEE IF YOU WERE OK.
CRUMB? IS THERE ANY WAY YOU CAN GET ME OUT OF HERE? PLEASE? I DON'T WANT TO END UP LIKE CHEF BONY BUTT IN HERE!
SHHH! IT BELONGS TO THE GHOST THAT HAUNTS THIS CELL. THAT'S WHY THEY PUT YOU IN HERE. SO YOU MIGHT GET SCARED INTO TELLING THEM WHAT THEY WANT TO KNOW.
BUT I DON'T KNOW ANYTHING! ONE MINUTE I WAS LOOKING FOR MY EARRING AND THEN POOF! HERE I AM.
THE QUEEN WANTS TO KNOW WHEN THE GREASE AND ALL THINGS IN IT ARE COMING BACK.

COMING BACK? SO YOU MEAN? HEY, WHAT'S WRONG?
GASP!

IT'S THE G...... THE G......

HEY, STOP! COME BACK! I NEED YOUR HELP!
GAAAAA!!!!!

HUH? WHAT'S HIS DEAL?

AHEM~

RRROAARR
EEEEEE!!

CRUMB MUST GET HELP!

HOW DO I GET OUT OF THIS?

YOU'LL WISH YOU NEVER CAME HERE, CHILD!

BUT I KEEP TELLING THEM IT'S NOT MY FAULT! WHY WON'T ANYONE BELIEVE ME? HERE HE COMES! I NEED A WEAPON.

THAT BONE!
HOPE THIS WORKS!
HEH HEH!
SWISH!
NO GOOD! IT JUST SLICED RIGHT THROUGH HIM!

TINK!
OH NO! HE'S GOT MY LEG!

AAAUGH!
FWAM!

GOTTA REACH THE SLOP BOWL!

RRARRRR!
STAY AWAY FROM ME!

CRASH!

HM?

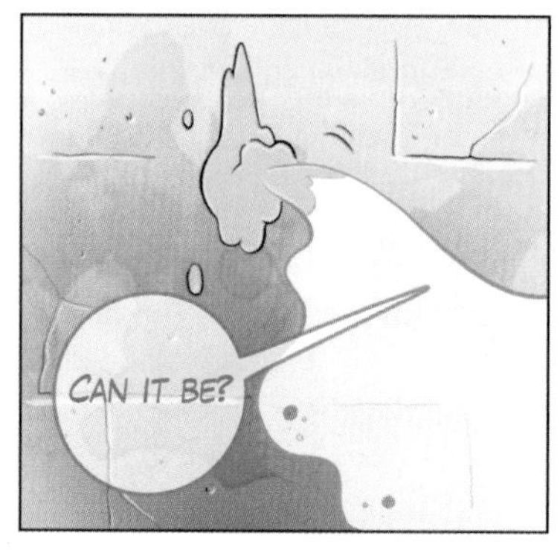
CAN IT BE?

HMMM.

BEH...STILL USING THE SAME OLD SLOP RECIPE. C'EST DOMMAGE.

SNIFF... U-UM...

A-ARE YOU GONNA...K-KILL ME?

MAIS NON, MA CHERIE! ALLOW ME TO INTRODUCE MYSELF. I AM THE GREAT CHEF GRISTLÉ AT YOUR SERVICE.

I AM VERY SORRY FOR SCARING YOU. I GET SO ANGRY WHEN GUARDS COME INTO MY CELL, I SOMETIMES CAN'T EVEN TELL WHO I'M SCARING.

PLEASE... ACCEPT THIS AS A TOKEN OF MY APOLOGIES.

WOW!
POOF!
ET VOILÀ! ONE PHANTOM BROCCOLI BUN!

POP!

MMM!

WOW, IT'S AMAZING! IT'S TASTY, AND I FEEL BETTER TOO!

LATER
SO WHY DID THEY THROW YOU IN HERE?
THE QUEEN THINKS THAT I'M SOMEHOW RESPONSIBLE FOR THE GREASE AND LEFTOVER SHORTAGE DOWN HERE.
AH LÀ LÀ! SO IT IS YOU WHO IS THE CAUSE OF THIS? THAT IS BAD...VERY BAD, EH?

IT'S NOT TRUE! UNTIL NOW I DIDN'T EVEN KNOW YOU GUYS EXISTED! I NEED TO GET OUT OF HERE SO I CAN PROVE MY INNOCENCE AND GO HOME. AT THIS RATE I'M NOT SURE WHO I'M GOING TO GET IT FROM WORSE, MY MOM OR THE QUEEN!
I CANT STAY HERE!!

BUT IT COULD BE NICE EH? KISS...KISS!
EW! I DON'T WANT TO BE A GREASY GHOST-WIFE!

EH, PERHAPS NOT. BUT NOW IT IS LATE, AND I MUST REST. SCARING PEOPLE IS HARD WORK.

WAIT!! YOU CAN'T JUST LEAVE ME LIKE THIS!

LISTEN CLOSELY, MA PETITE. THE WAY TO OBTAIN THE KEY TO FINDING YOUR WAY OUT OF HERE...

You must wipe the stripes!
Till we meet again.
Wipe the stripes? What's he talking about? I don't see anything that's striped. This is a riddle of some kind.
Wait a minute...
Those bars....
They make the light that's coming through look striped.
Can that be it?
I didn't think a ghost riddle could be so easy to solve. Maybe if I start here.
The texture seems rougher here.
PULL
"Pull?" Was this written in old slop? Ew! So what do I pull, I wonder.

?!
PULL
HMM...HOW DO I KNOW THIS ISN'T SOME KIND OF TRAP?
IS IT THIS FINGER THAT I NEED TO PULL?
THIS IS SO CREEPY! I'VE NEVER TOUCHED A REAL SKELETON BEFORE. I CAN'T DO IT!
HUMPH! GHOSTS? DON'T YOU KNOW THAT'S ALL A MYTH? THIS BETTER NOT BE SOME PRANK!
UH OH! I THINK I HEAR SOMEONE COMING.
WHAT IF...I JUST PULL IT...LIKE THIS?

BRAPPP!!

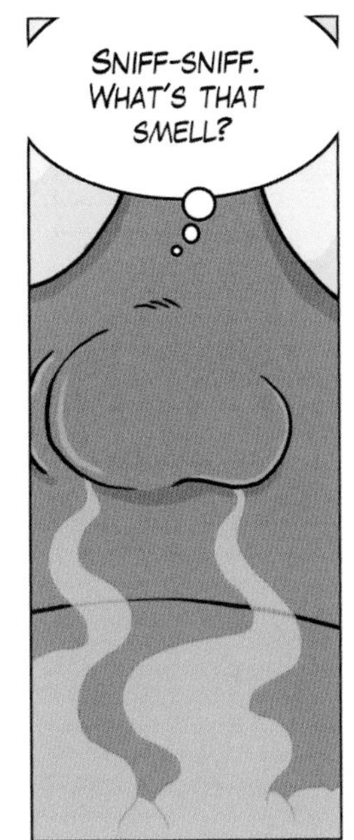
SNIFF-SNIFF. WHAT'S THAT SMELL?

OH NO! A GHOST FART! UNF...IT'S AWFUL!

HEY, WHAT'S THAT?

WOW! A SECRET DOOR JUST LIKE IN MY KNIGHT'S FIELD GAME!
RRRRRR

CRUMB, I SWEAR IF YOU WOKE ME UP FROM MY NAP OVER SOME NONSENSE, YOU'RE GOING TO BE THE NEXT GHOST IN HERE!
OH D-D-DEAR!
!

IT'S SO DARK. I CAN'T SEE ANYTHING.

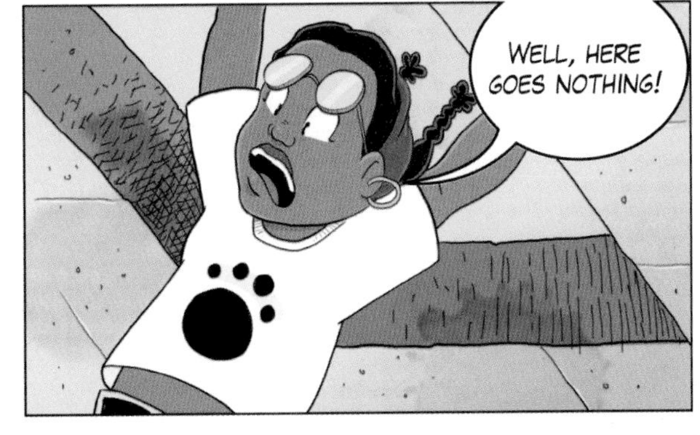
WELL, HERE GOES NOTHING!

RRRRRRR
Click
Clack!
Rise 'n' shine, Princess! Hyuck! Hyuck!
What the— GUARDS!!! The prisoner has ESCAPED!

WANTED

2000 GREASE-CRISPS

REWARD

HOPE IT'S WORTH IT!

AAAAAAAAAHHHH!

OOF!
THUNK!

WHAT THE... WHERE AM I?

WHAT IS THIS PLACE? IS THIS SOME KIND OF BUMPER CAR?

OW! WHAT'S THIS THING UNDER MY KNEE?

IT'S A WEIRD SHAPE.

IT LOOKS LIKE ONE OF THE MARSHMALLOWS THAT WERE IN THE CEREAL MOM USED TO BUY, BUT...

HELLOOO?! IS ANYBODY HOOOME?

HOME?
OME?
OME?

HISSS!!

SSCREEEEK!!
CRAZY ECHO IN HERE!
THERE'S NOBODY HERE. GUESS I'LL POCKET THIS WEIRD STONE AND GET MOVING.
WHOAH! WHAT WAS THAT SOUND?!
BOMF!
OUCH! HEY!! WHAT IS IT??
GET AWAY! GROSS...EVEN THE BATS HERE SMELL LIKE GREASE! WOOPS!!

YOWCH!! WHAT THE–?

I'M M-MOVING! WHAT DO I DO NOW?

I'M MOVING TOO FAST TO JUMP OUT! WHERE'S THE STEERING WHEEL ON THIS THING?
WELL...AT LEAST I GET TO LEAVE THOSE GREASE BATS BEHIND.
BUT WHAT'S UP AHEAD?
OH WELL...GUESS I'M GOING TO FIND OUT FIRST-HAND! GOOD THING MY STOMACH IS EMPTY!

Chapter 3
Friends in low places
'CAUSE THIS THING IS GOING EVEN FASTER NOW! HELP!!!
WARNING! BRIDGE OUT

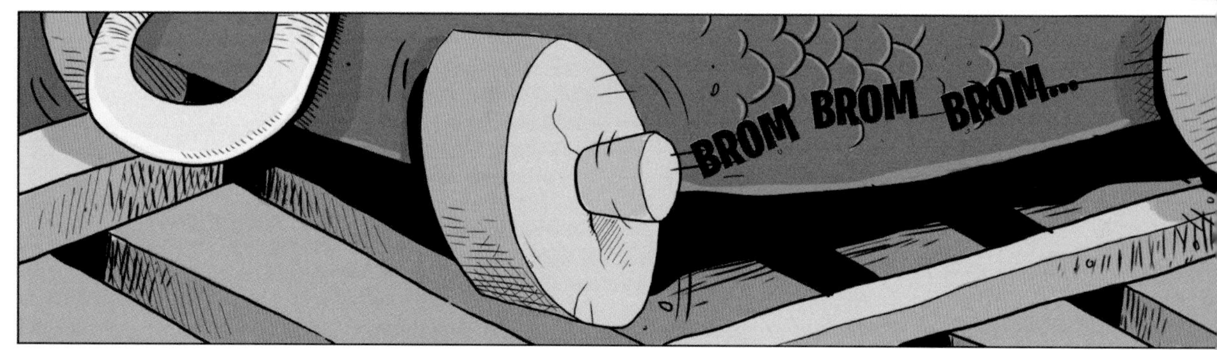
BROM BROM BROM...

EEEEEEEEHHH!!
YOU HEAR SOMETHING?
HUH?

UH-OH!! THE TRACK CUTS OFF, AND I CAN'T STOP!

AAAHHHH!!!

WHAAAAT?! YOU LET HER GET AWAY?!

SUCH INCOMPETENCE! YOU WOULDN'T EVEN MAKE A DECENT DISHWASHER!
I'M SORRY, MY QUEEN!
BE SILENT!

OOOOOOOH, I'M SO MAD I COULD JUST...

ERM...IF I MAY, YOUR MAJESTY?

HMM...
I BELIEVE THIS MIGHT BE A PERFECT JOB FOR OUR ROYAL RANGERS.

OH MY!! I JUST HAD THE MOST BRILLIANT IDEA! WE'LL GET THE ROYAL RANGERS TO RETRIEVE THAT MINCING LITTLE GIRL.

AHEM... ROYAL RANGERS!!!
ROYAL RANGERS...
ARE...
GO!
PLOOP!
!

WOOSH!!
THUMP!
TSSSS

ROYAL RANGERS! I HAVE BECKONED YOU HERE TO PERFORM A VITAL TASK. THERE IS AN INTRUDER IN THE KINGDOM, A YOUNG OVERLANDER. I WANT YOU TO BRING HER TO ME AT ONCE.
CHAR, YOUR FIGHTING SKILLS AND KNOWLEDGE OF POTIONS WILL BE HER DOOM.
CHUM, YOUR KNOWLEDGE OF TECHNOLOGY LETS YOU CREATE THE BEST TRAPS. IT'S A DONE DEAL.
AND CRUNCH, YOU'RE HALF BLOODHOUND AND HALF BRICK WALL. YOU THREE MUST BRING HER TO ME!
PIECE OF CAKE.
WE WILL NOT FAIL, YOUR MAJESTY.
THIS SHOULD BE FUN. HYUCK, HYUCK!

YOUR WISH IS OUR COMMAND.
HYA!
HYA!

POOF!

HEH HEH... HUH?
?!

DUH... GUYS?
GUYS?!

HMM...
HEY! WAIT UP, YOU GUYS!

Do you think they can pull it off?
My Queen, the Overlander could cause much harm. According the prophecy...she is destined to bring about the end of life as we know it. But even with all the tools at my disposal, I cannot see the answers.
We MUST find her and learn what she knows before she and the older Overlander can cause more damage to our people. The Haunted Cell failed to loosen her tongue. If she will not cooperate...then the Arena is the only other choice.
Leave it to me, your Majesty.
Ugh...am I still alive?

OH...MY BACK...AND MY FRONT...OUCH! LOOKS LIKE I'VE STOPPED AT LEAST.

IT'S SO DARK. THIS TORCH SHOULD HELP. DOES CRUMB LIGHT THESE, TOO?

W-WOW!

LOOKS LIKE NO ONE HAS BEEN THROUGH HERE IN AGES! I WONDER WHAT HAPPENED.

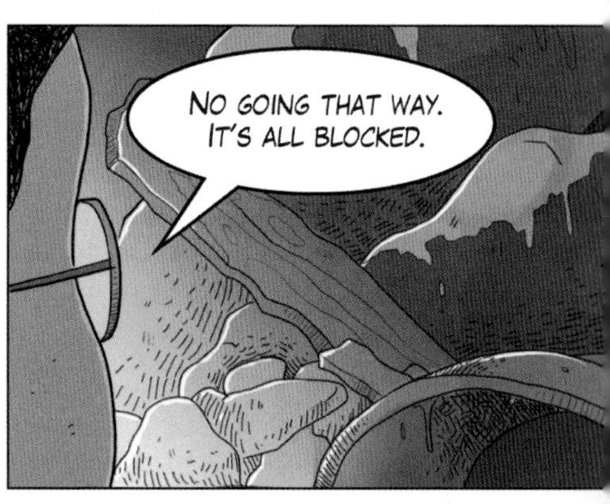
NO GOING THAT WAY. IT'S ALL BLOCKED.

IT LOOKS LIKE THIS GREASE STREAM IS RUNNING THE OTHER WAY.

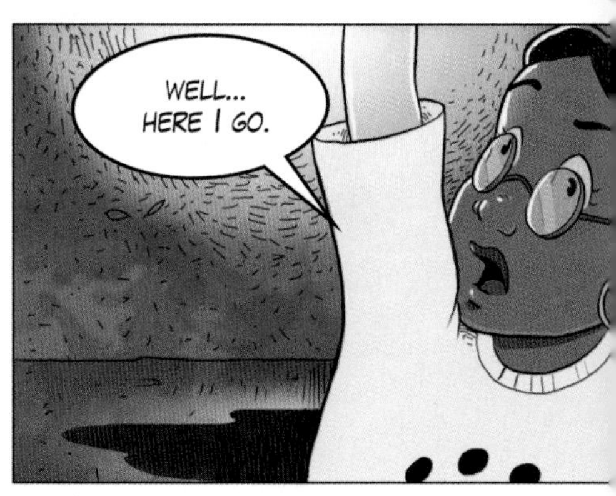
WELL... HERE I GO.

MEANWHILE, CRUMB HAS RETURNED TO THE HAUNTED CELL TO SEE IF HE CAN FIND ANY CLUES AS TO LILLY'S WHEREABOUTS.
ONLY THE SKELETON, BUT LILLY MA'AM DISAPPEARED LIKE A REAL GHOST!

HUH? WHAT'S THAT?

OH! SOME OF HER HEAD FUR IS ON IT!

WEL, WELL, WELL. WHAT HAVE WE HERE? HEH, HEH.
ULP!

HI! HI!
JUST WHAT ARE YOU UP TO, RUNT?
UH...

DIDJA RUN OUT OF TORCHES TO LIGHT OR GARBAGE TO DUMP? HYUCK-HYUCK!

LOOK HERE, DRUDGE, THIS IS A CRIME SCENE NOW! YOU HAVE NO BUSINESS BEING IN HERE.
UNLESS YOU ACTUALLY THINK YOU COULD DO OUR JOB.

WELL? CHUM ASKED YOU A QUESTION. YOU THINK YOU COULD BE A ROYAL RANGER?
HIM? DO OUR JOB? HA!
I... UH...

I'LL TELL YOU THE ANSWER. YOU COULD NEVER BE ANYTHING MORE THAN THE LOSER YOU ARE, BECAUSE YOU'RE NOTHING BUT A COWARDLY CRUMB!

NOW GET OUT! AND STAY OUT!!!

WHEW, MADE IT!
OOPS! OH HI.
SSSSSSS!

MAN, THIS TUNNEL GOES ON FOREVER. IT'S SO VAST AND EMPTY.
UGH...JUST LIKE MY STOMACH. SO HUNGRY!
GROOWWWLLLLLL.
IS THIS ALL PETRIFIED GREASE? I WONDER WHAT CAUSED THIS TO HAPPEN? THE AIR DOWN HERE IS COOLER. IT SMELLS CLEANER, TOO.
HOW LONG HAVE I BEEN DOWN IN THIS WORLD? LONG ENOUGH TO LOSE MY SCRUNCHIES.
NOW MY BRAIDS ARE COMING UNDONE.
IF MOM WERE HERE, SHE'D FIX THEM FOR ME AFTER MAKING ME SOMETHING TO EAT.
...MOM.
RIGHT NOW, ANYTHING SHE WOULD HAVE MADE WOULD SEEM LIKE A FEAST! THE LAST THING SHE MADE ME WAS CREAMY SQUASH SOUP WITH POTATOES AND LEEKS. I HATED TO ADMIT IT AT THE TIME, BUT IT WAS PRETTY TASTY.
HUMPH! GRUMBLE, MUMBLE.

MMM...I CAN ALMOST SMELL THE ROAST CHICKEN...

SNIFF!
...A-AND YOGURT WITH BERRIES FOR DESSERT. I CAN ALMOST SMELL THOSE FRESH, SUCCULENT BERRIES NOW.

WAIT A MINUTE. I REALLY DO SMELL BERRIES! WHAT'S THAT?!

OH, GREAT! ANOTHER MYSTERY DOOR. WAIT A SECOND. THAT SYMBOL.

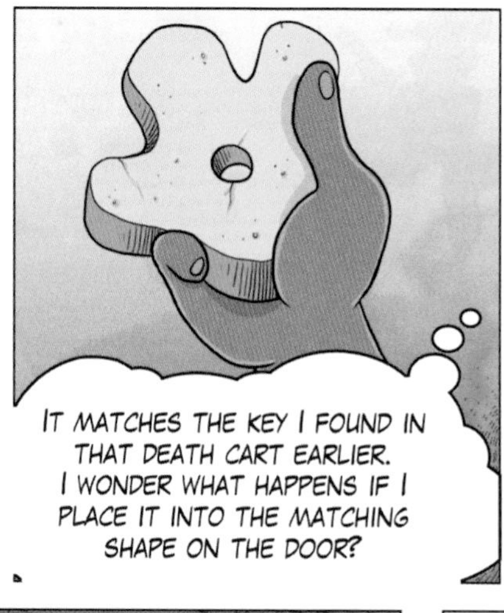
IT MATCHES THE KEY I FOUND IN THAT DEATH CART EARLIER. I WONDER WHAT HAPPENS IF I PLACE IT INTO THE MATCHING SHAPE ON THE DOOR?

OH! IT FITS PERFECTLY INTO THIS SHAPE.
CLACK

IT WORKED! THE DOOR IS OPENING!
RRRRRR.....

WHAT IF IT'S SOMETHING WORSE BEHIND HERE? BUT THAT SMELL IS EVEN STRONGER. I HAVE TO CHECK IT OUT.

I FEEL LIKE I READ A STORY ABOUT A GIRL WHO WENT THROUGH SOMETHING LIKE THIS ONCE.

OH WOOWWWWW!

THIS IS SO COOL!
LOOK AT THIS TREE!
THERE'S ALL KINDS OF WEIRD FRUIT GROWING ON IT. IT'S COMING THROUGH THE WALL, BUT IT LOOKS LIKE IT'S ROOTED IN THE WATER.
I WANT TO TRY ONE OF THESE FRUITS! IT LOOK LIKES A WATERMELON AND A PEAR!

LATER
HMMM...THESE ALL LOOK LIKE INSTRUCTIONS. THE PICTURES OF THE FOOD MATCHES A LOT OF THE THINGS I'M SEEING IN THIS CHAMBER.
MM...DELICIOUS! I WONDER WHO MADE ALL THIS STUFF.
WHOEVER WROTE THEM MUST LOVE FOOD AS MUCH AS I DO!
IT LOOKS LIKE THEY HAVE RECIPES ON THEM. COULD THE PERSON WHO LIVED HERE HAVE BEEN WORKING ON IMPROVING THE SLOP THEY SERVE TO BE HEALTHIER?

HUH? WHAT WAS THAT?
AHEM!

HELLO AGAIN, MON AMI!!!
COUGH! GAG! CHOKE!

MUCH LATER...
BUT CHEF, WHERE AM I? I FELT LIKE I WAS WALKING FOR MILES, AND THIS PLACE LOOKS TOTALLY DIFFERENT FROM EVERY OTHER!

THIS IS MY SECRET KITCHEN HIDEAWAY! RIGHT NOW WE ARE IN AN ABANDONED SECTION OF THE GREASE MINES. WHEN THE GREASE DRIED UP, IT BEGAN TO FALL APART, SO NO ONE COMES DOWN HERE ANYMORE.
IT WAS THE PERFECT PLACE FOR ME TO TRY MY COOKING EXPERIMENTS BEFORE I WAS CAPTURED.

YOU WERE TRYING TO CHANGE THE WAY YOU GUYS ATE TO A HEALTHIER WAY, RIGHT?
OUI! I WAS WORKING ON A PLAN TO COMPLETELY CHANGE THE WAY WE WERE EATING. OUR DIET OF GREASY SCRAPS IS SLOWLY DESTROYING MY PEOPLE, BUT SOMEONE HAD OTHER IDEAS.

YOU THINK SOMEONE STOPPED YOU ON PURPOSE? BUT WHO? AND WHY?
I THINK...

THAT THE ANSWER TO THAT QUESTION LIES IN UNDERSTANDING FRITE GASTRONOMY.

OH, FOR PETE'S SAKE! ANOTHER RIDDLE?! CAN'T YOU JUST GIVE STRAIGHT ANSWERS?
UM, I'D HAVE TO CHECK THE GHOST MANUAL FOR THAT.

HM? WHAT'S THAT SOUND? DO YOU HEAR IT?
SHHHHHHH! SOMEONE'S COMING!

QUICK! YOU HAVE TO DO SOMETHING!

WE MUST FIND A PLACE TO HIDE!

C-CRACK-KK!
THERE'S NO MORE TIME!

AAAAAH!
AAAAAHH!
CRASH!
HAHAHAHA! CRUMB! I NEVER THOUGHT I'D SEE YOU AGAIN!

UM, NICE TO SEE YOU, TOO. HEH-HEH.

WELCOME, MY FRIEND! HAVE A SLICE OF ECTO-EGGPLANT ANGEL FOOD CAKE!
CLICK!

WHOAH! IT'S OK, CRUMB. CHEF GRISTLÉ IS A FRIEND. HE WON'T HURT YOU. HOW'D YOU FIND US, ANYWAY?

WELL, CRUMB WENT BACK TO THE HAUNTED CELL TO TRY AND FIND OUT WHERE LILLY MA'AM HAD GONE.

CRUMB THOUGHT HE WAS ABOUT TO GET HIS FACE RIPPED OFF, BUT THEN...

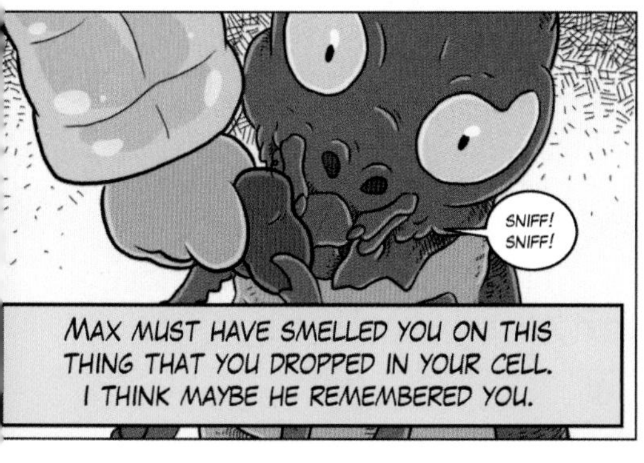
SNIFF! SNIFF!
MAX MUST HAVE SMELLED YOU ON THIS THING THAT YOU DROPPED IN YOUR CELL. I THINK MAYBE HE REMEMBERED YOU.

OMG... SO EMBARRASSING!
HE BONDED WITH YOU AFTER YOU UM...FED HIM IN THE QUEEN'S ROYAL CHAMBER.

THAT'S WHEN HE STARTED TO TRACK LILLY MA'AM'S SCENT, SO I GRABBED HIS LEASH.
WE TUNNELED DOWN, DOWN, DOWN THROUGH THE GROUND. DEEPER AND DEEPER INTO OUR WORLD... UNTIL WE ENDED UP FINDING YOU! LILLY MA'AM, YOU'RE IN DANGER! THE QUEEN HAS SENT THE ROYAL RANGERS TO GO AND FIND YOU!

AH, BUT THIS IS VERY BAD! IF THE ROYAL RANGERS HAVE BEEN SENT OUT, IT WON'T BE LONG BEFORE THEY FIND YOU!
YOU MUST LEAVE HERE QUICKLY! EVEN MY HIDEAWAY ISN'T SAFE!
HE'S RIGHT! THEY NEVER MISS WHEN IT COMES TO FINDING THEIR TARGET. WE HAVE TO GET OUT OF HERE!
I WILL HOLD THEM OFF UNTIL YOU CAN GET AWAY!
WHO IN BLAZES ARE THE ROYAL RANGERS? AND HOW DOES CHEF MAKE HIMSELF ALL PUFFY LIKE THAT?
MAX, CAN YOU HELP FIND US A PLACE WHERE WE'LL BE SAFE FROM THE ROYAL RANGERS? GOOD BOY!
WAIT, MA CHERIÉ! TAKE THIS BOOK WITH YOU! IT WILL HELP YOU IN MORE WAYS THAN ONE!
HUH?
WHAT IS THIS? UGH, I BET IT'S CHEF GRISTLÉ'S BIG BOOK OF UN-FUNNY RIDDLES. WHY ME?
LILLY MA'AM, WE HAVE TO GO!
THIS BOOK IS HEAVY! WHY CAN'T YOU CARRY IT?
MY ARMS ARE TOO SHORT.

YOU SUMMONED ME, ADVISOR?
YES, CHAR. HAVE YOU FOUND THE GIRL YET?
NOT YET, SIR. BUT THE OTHER TWO HAVE PICKED UP HER TRAIL. WE WILL SOON HAVE HER.

TIME IS RUNNING OUT.

YES, SIR.

AS SOON AS YOU GET HER YOU **MUST** BRING HER TO ME **UNHARMED.** IT IS VITAL THAT I FIND OUT WHAT SHE KNOWS.

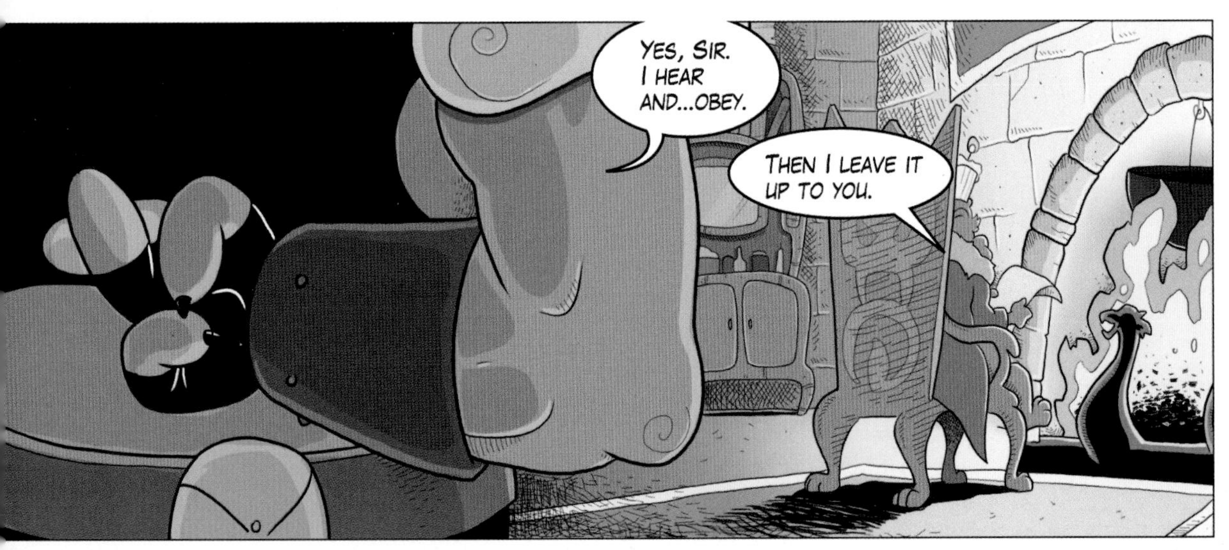
YES, SIR. I HEAR AND...OBEY.
THEN I LEAVE IT UP TO YOU.

The
Royal
Ovenland
CREST

Chapter 4

Fight or flight

MEANWHILE, ARMED ONLY WITH A RECIPE BOOK CHOCK FULL OF SECRETS, LILLY, CRUMB, AND MAX JOURNEY THROUGH THE UNCHARTED DEPTHS OF OVENLAND.
SO, WHERE ARE WE, CRUMB? IT FEELS LIKE WE'VE BEEN WALKING FOR DAYS.
DEEP IN THESE TUNNELS THERE ARE MANY PATHS THAT GO TO MANY PLACES. SOME SAY THAT OTHER OVENLANDS CAN EVEN BE REACHED.
THERE ARE ALSO MULTIPLE ENTRYWAYS INTO YOUR WORLD, LILLY-MA'AM. MANY, MANY DOORS.

IT'S SO HOT. I'D SUFFER HAVING TEA WITH THE QUEEN FOR A GLASS OF COLD WATER.

IF WE CONTINUE THIS WAY, IT SHOULD TAKE US VERY CLOSE TO LILLY-MA'AM'S HOUSE.

CRUMB, DO YOU MEAN THAT I CAN GET HOME THIS WAY?

SMART THINKING, CRUMB!
MAX, KEEP AN EYE OUT FOR ANYTHING SUSPICIOUS.

I SURE HOPE WE CAN MAKE IT BEFORE THOSE GOOFY GUARDS CATCH US.

SNIF! SNIF!
HMMMM. I THNK I'VE PICKED UP THE SCENT OF THAT INFERNAL OVERLANDER.

CHUM! USE YOUR SPECIAL GREASE GOGGLES TO SEE IF YOU CAN PICK UP ANY SIGNS OF THOSE THREE.
YESSIR!

LET'S SEE NOW...

ALERT! UNKNOWN GREASE SIGNATURE DETECTED!
GOT SOMETHING! THESE TRACKS ON THE LEFT ARE DEFINITELY NOT FROM ANY OF US.

THIS HAS TO BE THEM, SIR! THESE GOGGLES NEVER LIE.

OK THEN, WE MUST BE CLOSE. SET UP A PERIMETER SO THEY CAN'T ESCAPE.
CRUNCH, STOP EATING THOSE GREASE CRISPS AND GET READY TO EXECUTE ATTACK PATTERN SPICY BATTER-ING RAM!

OOF! MY FEET ARE **KILLING** ME! LET'S STOP FOR A SECOND.

IN THESE UNUSED TUNNELS, THE GREASE NO LONGER FLOWS. THE WATER FROM ABOVE IS ALL THAT FLOWS FROM THESE FOUNTAINS NOW.
HEY, CRUMB, WHAT'S THAT?

SO THE FARTHER WE GET FROM THE MAIN KINGDOM, THE WEAKER THE GREASE FLOW!

SLURRRP!
AMAZING: THIS WATER ISN'T ALL YUCKY AND GREASY.

FEELS GREAT TO **FINALLY** COOL OFF.

AHH... THAT FEELS **SO** MUCH BETTER!

UH-OH! I FORGOT WHAT HAPPENS WHEN...
RRKRUMMBBLE

THERE'S TOO MUCH HUMIDITY.
FLOOF!

SIGH, GREASE-EVERYTHING IN THIS PLACE, BUT NO GREASE-COMB. I GUESS FINGER COMBING WILL HAVE TO SUFFICE.
HEY, CRUMB, GETTING ANYTHING USEFUL OUT OF THAT BOOK, YET?
LOOKS LIKE MAX IS GETTING HIS DAILY FIBER ALLOWANCE.
CRUMB LEARNED MANY GLYPHS IN SECRET AFTER HIS CHORES WERE DONE, BUT THESE ARE VERY OLD, SO IT'S HARDER TO UNDERSTAND THEM.
ON THIS SIDE, IT TALKS ABOUT THE MAIN FOCUS OF OUR DIET: THE GREASE AND CRISPY BITS AND CHUNKS THAT FLOWED INTO OUR WORLD.
IT ALSO ENCOURAGED US TO BE BRAVE AND SEEK THESE TREASURES NEAR THE ENTRANCE TO OUR WORLD.
ON THE RIGHT SIDE IT'S DIFFERENT. IT STARTS TALKING ABOUT SOME KIND OF PROPHECY...A DANGER THAT THREATENS US IF WE DON'T START TO BRANCH OFF AND START TO MOVE AWAY FROM OUR WAYS OF EATING THE WAY WE DO.
THEN IT SAYS... GASP!!!
MUNCH MUNCH
GASP? THAT DOESN'T SOUND GOOD. WHAT DOES IT SAY NEXT?!
WELL?? WHAT?

KA-BOOM!
SNORT!
YOW!!!

CLOP!

OOF! WHAT THE--?
RUN, CRUMB!

HA! HA! HA! HA! HA! HA! HA!

OHH, MY HEAD. THIS IS GETTING RIDICULOUS.

HUH? WHERE AM I?
ENJOY YOUR NAP? HEH, HEH.

YOU'RE IN THE ROYAL RANGERS' RUMPUS ROOM, AND WE'VE BROUGHT YOU HERE TO DEAL WITH YOU ONCE AND FOR ALL.
BUT I WASN'T TRYING TO DO ANYTHING, I SWEAR! I WAS JUST TRYING TO FINISH MY CHORES!

SHADDAP AND PAY ATTENTION, YA HEAR?

BECAUSE YOU'RE ABOUT TO GET AN OFFER YOU CAN'T REFUSE! HI! HI!

LISTEN UP, OVERLANDER! WE ROYAL RANGERS HAVE A PROUD AND ILLUSTRIOUS HISTORY OF GOING ABOVE TO YOUR WORLD AND RISKING OUR LIVES TO BRING BACK AS MUCH OF YOUR GREASY, CRISPY, CRUNCHY REFUSE AS POSSIBLE. AT ANY MOMENT WE COULD HAVE BEEN SPOTTED, BUT WE WERE TOO STEALTHY.
FOR YEARS WE TRAIN FOR THE RIGHT TO HOLD THIS POST. MANY NEVER MAKE IT.
LONG LIVE THE ROYAL RANGERS!
HEE!HEE!
WE WERE CHEERED AS HEROES! FRITES SING SONGS ABOUT US! NOW THAT THERE'S EVEN LESS OF THAT FOOD THAN EVER BEFORE, OUR PEOPLE'S NEED FOR US HAS INCREASED. WE'VE BEEN UPGRADED TO MORE THAN JUST HEROES.

I'VE ALREADY HEARD THE QUEEN'S ADVISOR MUMBLING ABOUT SOME PROPHECY. YOU MEAN TO END OUR NOBLE CAREERS, BUT I WON'T ALLOW THAT.

CRUNCH! OPEN THE GATE!

KKRRRRRR...
NNNGH...

GASP! IS THAT...

HEH, HEH. KNOW WHAT THIS IS?

THIS IS THE TUNNEL THAT TAKES US TO YOUR WORLD. IT LEADS RIGHT TO WHERE WE CONDUCTED MOST OF OUR RAIDS. YOUR KITCHEN.
THIS IS YOUR FIRST AND LAST CHANCE.

PROMISE TO LEAVE AND NEVER RETURN AND WE WILL LET YOU FREE. STEP INTO THE TUNNEL, AND TONIGHT YOU CAN SLEEP IN YOUR OWN BED, INSTEAD OF A CELL.

B-BUT...

WHAT ABOUT CRUMB?

HEE! HEE! HEE! WHAT ABOUT HIM? HE'S ALREADY IN ENOUGH TROUBLE FOR HELPING AN OVERLANDER.
WHY NOT WORRY ABOUT YOURSELF?

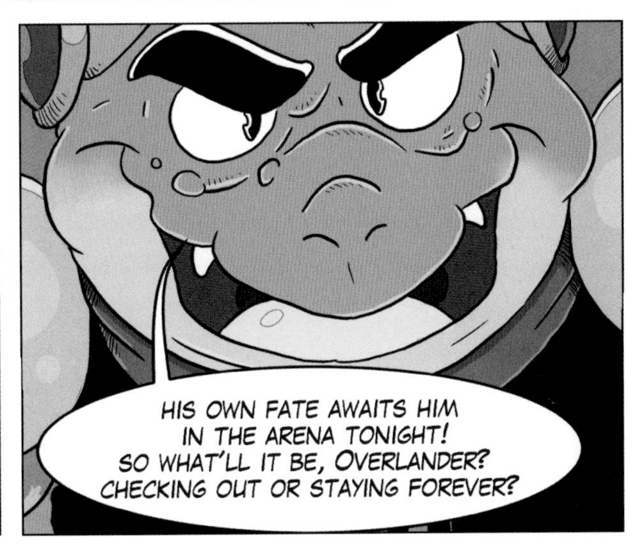
HIS OWN FATE AWAITS HIM IN THE ARENA TONIGHT! SO WHAT'LL IT BE, OVERLANDER? CHECKING OUT OR STAYING FOREVER?

WHAT DO I DO? I CAN LEAVE RIGHT NOW BUT...
BUT HE HELPED ME WHEN I NEEDED HELP.

I...

I'LL GO.

UNTIE HER.
OK, LILLY-CHAN, THINK FAST!

THAT MUST BE HOW WE CAME IN.

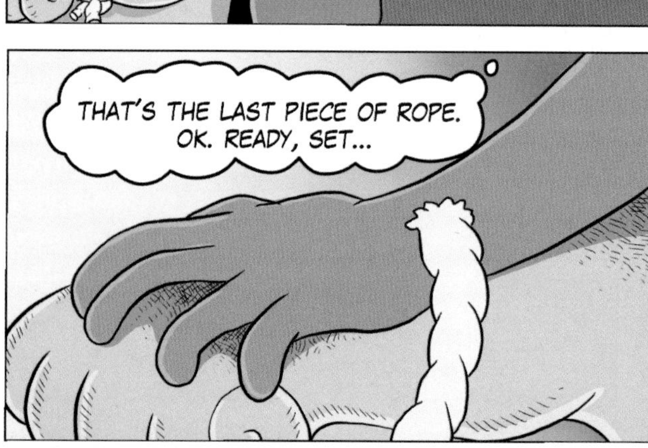
THAT'S THE LAST PIECE OF ROPE. OK. READY, SET...

GO!
HEY!

NNNNGH!!!
I CAN'T BUDGE IT.

GASP!

LILLY VISION
STOMP!
STOMP!

SMASH!

OUT COLD
AGAIN? SHEESH.
DO THESE GUYS
GET BENEFITS?

COME BACK HERE! CHUM, PUT DOWN THAT STUPID GREASE GUN!

NOOOO! GET HER, YOU FOOLS!!!

WHICH WAY DO I GO?! EENY MEENY MINY...

MO!

SHE WENT THIS WAY!

GEEZ, LOUISE, NOW WHAT DO I DO?

H-HUH?

MAX! YOU FOUND ME! GLAD TO SEE YOU, BOY! GOOD BOY!

NOW, MAX, PAY CLOSE ATTENTION. YOU REMEMBER CRUMB, RIGHT?

STINKY
CRUMB
HISSSSSSS!

AW, COME ON. DON'T BE LIKE THAT. HE'S ALWAYS BEEN NICE TO US, RIGHT? NOW HE NEEDS OUR HELP.
I'M NOT SURE WE CAN DO IT ALONE, THOUGH.

WE NEED HELP TO RESCUE HIM. ANY IDEAS FOR WHO WE CAN HIT UP?

POOF!
THAT'S IT! WE NEED CHEF!

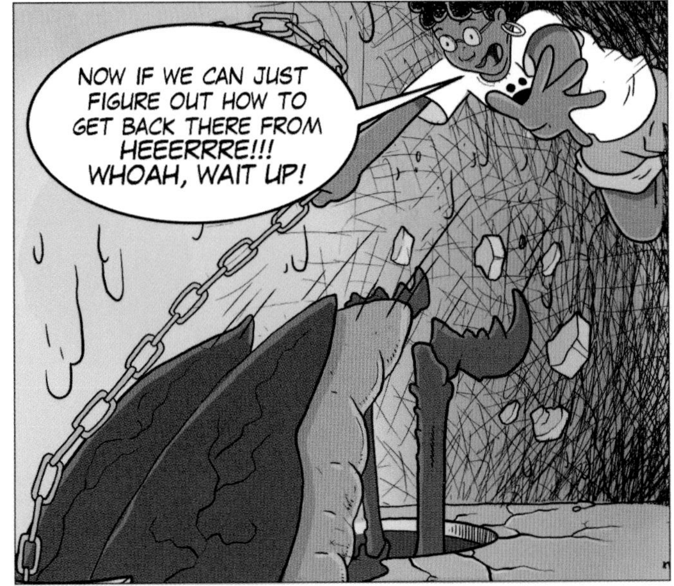
NOW IF WE CAN JUST FIGURE OUT HOW TO GET BACK THERE FROM HEEERRRE!!! WHOAH, WAIT UP!

AHHHH...
I LOVE FRY-DAY NITE FRITE FIGHTS. EVERYTHING GETS SO PEACEFUL AND QUIET. I CAN PERFECT MY GHOSTLY RECIPES IN PEACE AND QUIET!

HMM? WHAT'S THAT NOISE?

WHAT'S THIS? MY FRIEND HAS RETURNED SO SOON?
OOF!

CHEF, WE NEED YOUR HELP! CRUMB IS IN TROUBLE!

HMPH!
WHY SHOULD I HELP? IT IS FRITES THAT GOT ME INTO MY SITUATION IN THE FIRST PLACE!
BUT NOT ALL FRITES WERE MEAN TO YOU. CRUMB WAS JUST SCARED. PLEASE!

HMM...I HAVE AN IDEA. BUT I NEED SOME OF THE RECIPES FROM THAT BOOK I GAVE TO YOU.

BUT THE ROYAL RANGERS TOOK THAT WHEN THEY GRABBED ME.
ISN'T THERE ANYTHING ELSE WE CAN USE?

BUT THOSE RECIPES WERE SPECIAL, AND ONLY I POSSESS THE NEEDED INGEDIENTS! FRITE DIRECT DOESN'T REALLY DELIVER DOWN HERE, YOU KNOW?

NOW WHAT WILL WE DO?

?
COUGH! HACK!

EW! WHAT THE...
HACK!

GROSS! HEY, CHEF, THESE MUST BE THE PAGES HE ATE OUT OF THE BOOK EARLIER.

BUT THIS IS GOOD! WE CAN USE THESE PAGES FOR MY PLAN!

NOW, MA CHERIE, IF YOU ARE GOING INTO BATTLE FOR YOUR FRIEND, YOU A NEED A UNIFORM MORE SUITED TO THIS.
LOOK BEHIND THAT CURTAIN THERE.
BATTLE?

THIS CHEST BACK HERE?

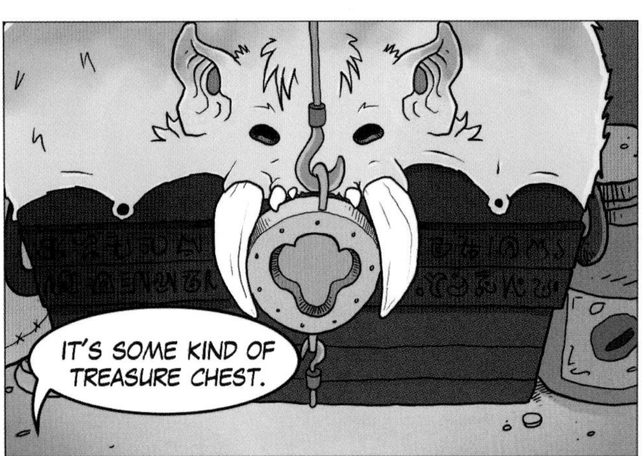
IT'S SOME KIND OF TREASURE CHEST.

THAT STONE I FOUND FITS THIS SHAPE PERFECTLY.
CLACK!

OHHH. IT'S FILLED WITH BEAUTIFUL THINGS!

WHY DO YOU HAVE ALL THIS STUFF, CHEF?

I USED TO WORK AS A STYLIST ON DANCING WITH THE FRITES!
AirFlo 2000
NOW, WE MUST HURRY. THERE IS NOT MUCH TIME!

YOU GOT THAT RIGHT, CHEF!
LADIES AND GENTLEFRITES!

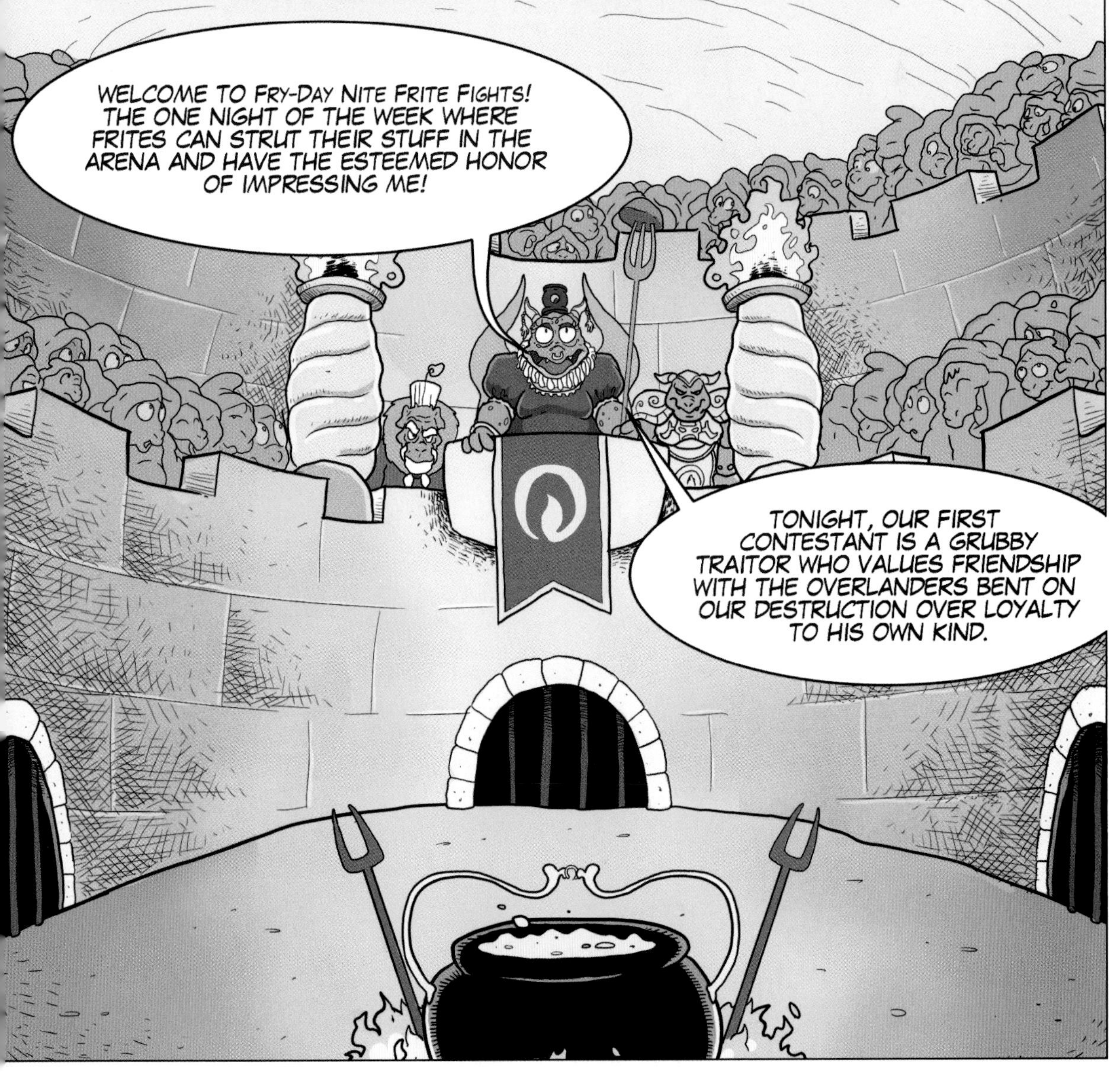
WELCOME TO FRY-DAY NITE FRITE FIGHTS! THE ONE NIGHT OF THE WEEK WHERE FRITES CAN STRUT THEIR STUFF IN THE ARENA AND HAVE THE ESTEEMED HONOR OF IMPRESSING ME!
TONIGHT, OUR FIRST CONTESTANT IS A GRUBBY TRAITOR WHO VALUES FRIENDSHIP WITH THE OVERLANDERS BENT ON OUR DESTRUCTION OVER LOYALTY TO HIS OWN KIND.

LET'S START WITH OUR FIRST GAME OF THE EVENT.
THE CRISP AND THE PENDULUM!

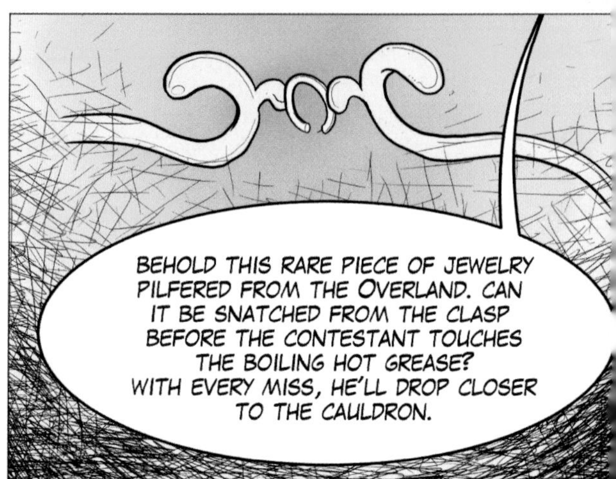
BEHOLD THIS RARE PIECE OF JEWELRY PILFERED FROM THE OVERLAND. CAN IT BE SNATCHED FROM THE CLASP BEFORE THE CONTESTANT TOUCHES THE BOILING HOT GREASE? WITH EVERY MISS, HE'LL DROP CLOSER TO THE CAULDRON.

LOWER THE CONESTANT!

HISS!
BOO!
HA! HA!
GRAB THE GOLD RING?
OR A DEEP-FRIED FATE?
WHICH SHALL IT BE?

LET'SEE IF THIS LOWLY SUBJECT CAN BE AS CLEVER AT FREEING HIMSELF...

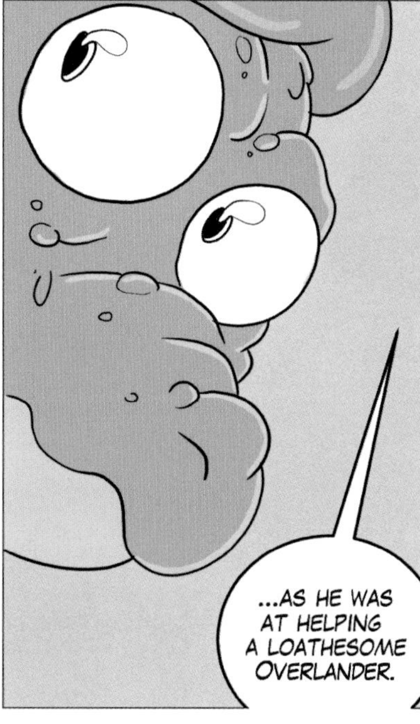
...AS HE WAS AT HELPING A LOATHESOME OVERLANDER.

BEGIN THE GAMES!!!

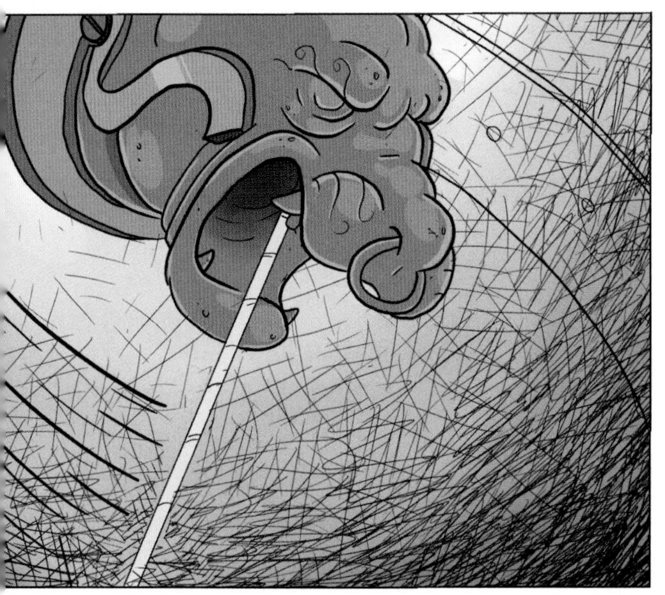

GAH! I MISSED IT! CRUMB'S COORDINATION IS SO BAD DESPITE SO MANY GAMES OF SOLO GREASE PONG!

IT FEELS SO HOT AND CRUMB GETTING CLOSER...

WHAT WILL CRUMB DO?

STOP!

WHO'S THAT?
HUH?
HEY! GET OFF!

WHY, YOU LITTLE...
YOU'VE CERTAINLY CHANGED FROM THE WINGING LITTLE WORM I SPOKE TO EARLIER! NOW WE'LL REALLY PUT YOUR NEWFOUND COURAGE TO THE TEST!
QUEEN ADIPOSSERIA! IT'S TIME TO STOP YOUR BULLYING OF MY FRIEND! IT'S TRUE...I AM AN OVERLANDER, BUT I'M ALSO INNOCENT OF THE THINGS YOU ACCUSE ME OF. IT SEEMS CRUMB IS FAIRER IN HIS THINKING. MAYBE HE'D MAKE A BETTER RULER THAN YOU!
ANYTHING YOU CAN DISH OUT, I CAN... HEY! THAT'S...
MY EARRING!!!

ALL THIS TIME I'VE BEEN RUNNING AROUND LIKE SOME CUT-RATE PIRATE WITH ONE EARRING! MY MOM GAVE ME THAT. NOW I'M REALLY MAD!

YOU'RE FAR TOO OVERCONFIDENT, LITTLE ONE.
I WON'T LET YOU GET AWAY WITH THIS, QUEEN.

STRANGE... THIS OVERLANDER LOOKS DIFFERENT SOMEHOW... ALMOST LIKE...
HEH, HEH.

NOW I'LL SHOW YOU!

RELEASE THE MIGHTY SNAGGLORD!!!

SNAGGLORD? WHAT'S A SNAGGLORD?
KREEE
RRRRR......
GGRAWWRR!
!!!

WHAT IS THAT THING? A MUTANT PIZZA RAT?!

I NEED A WEAPON! OH! OVER THERE!

GOTTA MOVE!

NGH! I CAN'T MOVE IT!

!

EAT THIS, RAT FACE!

CRUNCH
YIKES!

NO! DON'T EAT ME! I'M NOT BATTER-DIPPED!

HELP!!!

?!

RRR...
HISSSS!
MAX?

THWAK!
WHOAH!

HE'S FLYING BACK AROUND! WAIT, HE'S COMING TOWARD... ME!
HEY! MAX, WHAT ARE YOU DOING?
YOW! NOW I GET IT! DON'T DROP ME!

IMPOSSIBLE! TOGETHER THEY ALMOST RESEMBLE...

THE IMAGE OF THE PROPHECY FROM THIS GASTRONOMY BOOK THAT CHAR BROUGHT TO ME.

WE'RE COMING, CRUMB! HOLD OUT YOUR HAND!

LILLY-MA'AM!

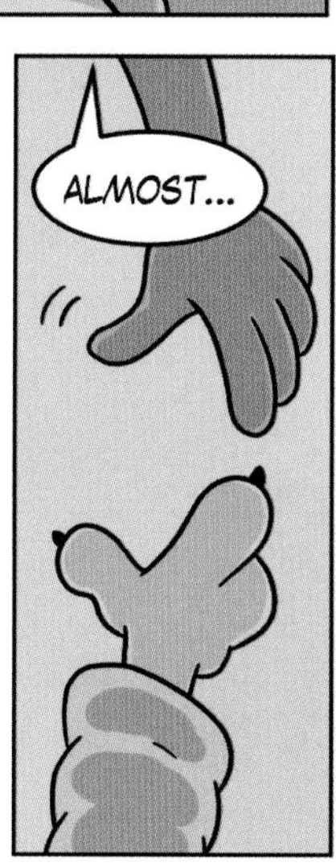
ALMOST...

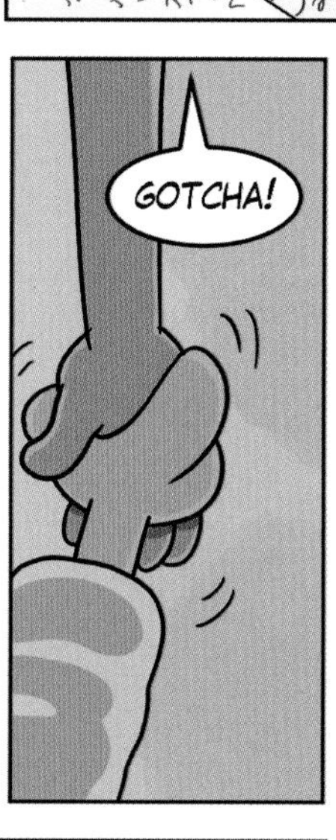
GOTCHA!

HANG ON, CRUMB! TRY TO GET HIGHER, MAX!

WUH-OH, HE LOOKS LIKE HE'S ABOUT TO TRY SOMETHING.

GULP! I WAS RIGHT!

CHOMP!

CREEEEEE!
AAAAAH!
FWAM!
OH NO...
GRRRAAAA
I'M DONE FOR!
BONJOUR!
POOF
!
CHEF! I THOUGHT YOU'D NEVER GET HERE!

TRY MY MINI BROCCOLI BRIOCHE, MY RATTY FRIEND!
POP!
CHOMP! CHOMP!
CHEF, CAN YOU FLY UP AND TRY TO FREE CRUMB?
BUT OF COURSE!
WOOSH!
HERE! TRY MY FRUITS AND TASTY VEGETABLE TREATS!
YUM!
THESE TASTE KIND OF GOOD!
MMM... THESE AREN'T MADE WITH CRISPS?

HELLO! MIND IF I, UH, HANG OUT WITH YOU? HI, HI, HI!

DON'T LOOK SO SOUR!

THWAK!
MY SPIRIT SPATULA WILL CUT YOU LOOSE!

OOPS... I FORGOT ABOUT GRAVITY!
AAAAAH!
BOMP!

OOF!

OH, HI! HEH, HEH?
GRRRR...

BETTER DO SOMETHING FAST!

HEY, RAT FACE! WANT ANOTHER TASTY TREAT?

C'MON, BOY!

FETCH IT!

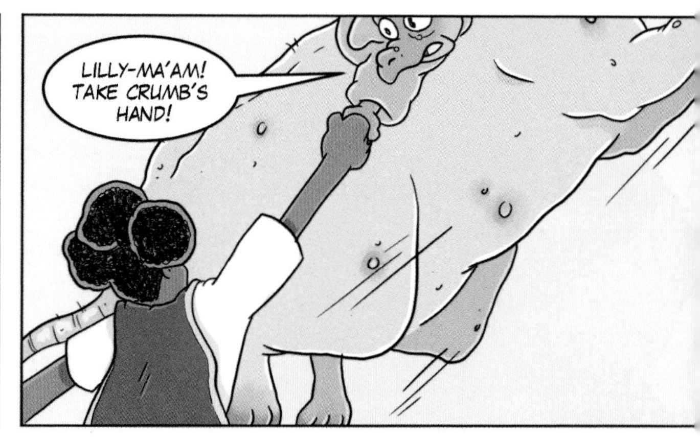
LILLY-MA'AM! TAKE CRUMB'S HAND!

THIS IS OUTRAGEOUS! WHAT'S GOING ON? WHY ISN'T SNAGGLORD CHOMPING THAT GIRL? WHY CAN'T I HAVE A SNACK?!

POP!
MY QUEEN...
WHY CAN'T... UH OH.

CRASH!

WHOA. ARE WE STOPPED?

HAVE NO FEAR, THE ROYAL RANGERS ARE HERE, YOUR MAJESTY!
HEE! HEE! HEE! HERE TO SAVE THE DAY!
HEY! GET OFF!

HUH? WHEN DID YOU GUYS GET HERE? WELL, YOU BETTER BACK OFF IF YOU KNOW WHAT'S GOOD FOR YOU!

ALL I HAVE TO DO IS TOSS THIS TREAT ONTO THE QUEEN'S FACE, AND SNAGGLORD WILL CHOMP THE WHOLE THING!

TIME'S RUNNING OUT, CHAR! NOW, TELL THE TRUTH...
sniff!
sniff!

WHAT DID YOU DO TO THE KING OF OVENLAND?

ALL RIGHT, IT WAS ME! I DID IT! I SPIKED THE CHEF'S FIRST ATTEMPT AT ADDING HEALTHY FOOD TO THE ROYAL DIET!
LUNCHTIME, YOUR MAJESTY!

ALL IT TOOK WAS A PINCH OF MINYOO POWDER AND POOF! THE KING WAS TRANSFORMED. I KNEW THE CHEF WOULD BE BLAMED AND WE'D BE SURE TO GO BACK TO OUR OLD WAY OF EATING AND LIVING! OUR FUTURE WAS SECURED.
POOF!
CHAR, ARE YOU SAYING...
GBLTHHHRRRL

THAT IT WAS YOU THE WHOLE TIME? YOU ALLOWED US TO THINK THAT TRYING DIFFERENT FOODS WOULD BE DANGEROUS?

YES! IT WAS ME! DON'T YOU UNDERSTAND? WE CAN'T CAN'T START EATING THIS STUFF WITHOUT PAYING A PRICE! THE ROYAL RANGERS WERE ALWAYS MEANT TO DO WHAT WE DO. WE'RE SUPPOSED TO BE HEROES... FOREVER!!! WE WERE MEANT TO EAT GREASY, GOBBY GOODNESS!

WOW!
THIS IS SO
JUICY!
YUM!
THIS IS
SWEET!

HEY, QUEEN!
CATCH!

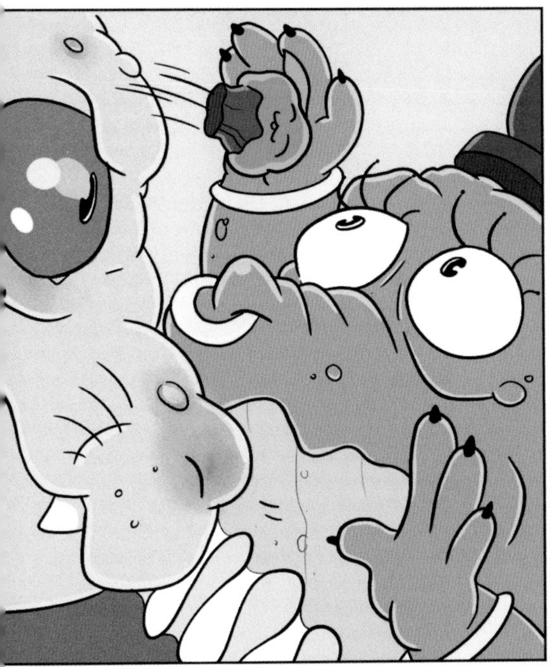

HMMM...
NOT BAD. IS IT POSSIBLE
THAT I COULD HAVE BEEN...
WRONG?!

GUARDS!!!
COME HAUL THIS BEAST OFF
OF ME! I HAVE A GHOST CHEF
I NEED TO APOLOGIZE TO!

LATER...
WELL, HERE WE ARE. BACK IN THE RUMPUS ROOM.
YES, LILLY-MA'AM. YOU CAN GO HOME NOW.

ARE YOU GOING TO BE OK, CRUMB?
YES, CRUMB THINKS SO. NOW THAT EVERYONE KNOWS WHAT THE ROYAL RANGERS DID, THEY'VE BEEN THROWN IN THE DUNGEON

THEY WON'T BOTHER CRUMB ANYMORE
BOSS, I'M HUNGRY!
SHADDAP!
HEE! HEE! HEE!

AND BESIDES, NOW THAT CRUMB IS AN APPRENTICE TO CHEF GRISTLÉ, EVERY FRITE IS NICER.
THE ADVISOR AND QUEEN WANT TO SEE WHAT ELSE WE CAN MAKE THAT'S TASTY!

THAT'S GREAT, CRUMB! WELL, I GUESS THIS IS IT.

HERE I GO.

LILLY-MA'AM, WAIT! I ALMOST FORGOT TO GIVE YOU THIS!

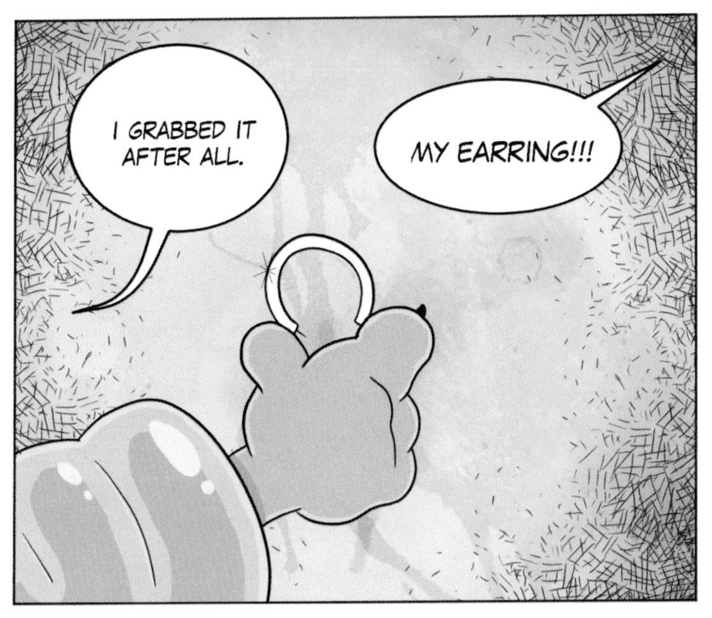
MY EARRING!!!
I GRABBED IT AFTER ALL.

I'M GOING TO MISS YOU, CRUMB. YOU WERE A FRIEND TO ME FROM THE VERY START.

BE GOOD, MAX. TAKE CARE OF THAT LEG, AND, UH...DON'T EAT ANY MORE BARF.

LATER, YOU GUYS!

ZOOP!

HOME. I CAN'T BELIEVE IT.
I ACTUALLY MADE IT BACK FROM THAT GREASY, MESS MADHOUSE.
LOOKS LIKE THE COAST IS CLEAR.
BANG!

NOW, IF I CAN JUST GET CLEANED UP BEFORE... WUH-OH.

LILLY BROWN! WHAT DO YOU THINK YOU'RE DOING PLAYING AROUND IN MY OVEN? HAVE YOU EVEN DONE ANY OF YOUR CHORES?!!!

AND WHO ARE YOU SUPPOSED TO BE? PRINCESS CRUSTY OVEN OR SOMETHING?I CAN'T BELIEVE THAT THIS IS WHAT YOU'VE BEEN UP TO ALL THIS TIME!

M-MOM?

MOM, WOULD YOU MAKE ME SOME OF THAT EGGPLANT STUFF? A-AND MAYBE SOME TURKEY CHILI WITH RICE? PLEEEAAASE?
B-BUT I THOUGHT YOU HATED MY EGGPLANT PUREE!

GREAT JOB CLEANING UP THE APARTMENT, LILLY, BUT AFTER WE GET DONE WITH THIS FEAST, I'M GOING TO NEED YOUR HELP GETTING ALL THESE DISHES CLEANED.
SURE THING, MOM. JUST KEEP THIS YUMMY SRIRACHA AND EGGPLANT, TOFU BAKE COMING. I'LL DO THE DISHES!
AND I'LL WAX THE FLOOR AFTER...
A-AND THEN I'LL DO THE LAUNDRY!
AND AFTER THAT, I'LL SEPARATE ALL THE RECYCLING.
AND DIDN'T YOU SAY YOU NEED THE RUGS TO BE SHAMPOOD?
THE END

MALICE IN OVENLAND COVER ART

Malice
in
OVENLAND

Malice
in
OVENLAND

Malice
in
Ovenland

Malice
in
OVENLAND

CHARACTER PROFILE PAGE

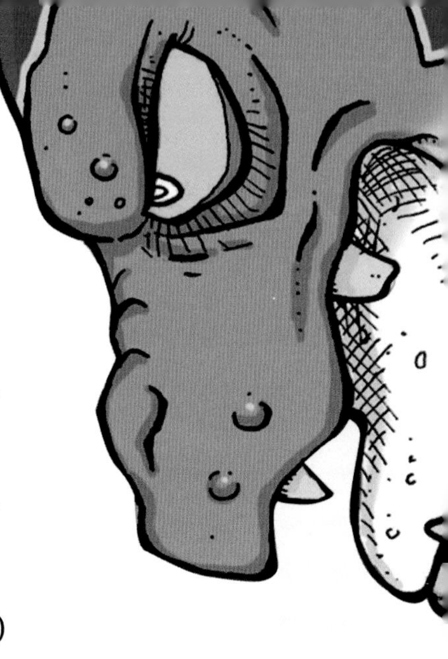

I sit down with the Captain of the Ovenland Queen's Royal Guard to find out more about him.

M.Hess: Hello! Thank you for taking time to speak with us today. I'm sure you must be very busy and–

Captain: YEAH! YEAH.....Make it snappy, will ya? (burp!)

M.Hess: Well uh...Certainly! So tell me, what's your real name?

Captain: Sherbet.

M.Hess: Sh-Sherbet? Like the dessert? (Snicker)

Captain: ARE YOU LAUGHIN' AT ME, WIMP?

M.Hess: No, no! Not at all! So tell me...How did you manage to become the Captain of the Queens Royal Guard?

Captain: I achieved it by workin' hard, bein' brave, and by givin' the old Captain a spoiled bowl of Chef's Gloppy Gruel...hyuk! hyuk! hyuk!

M.Hess: I uh...I see..So, do you have any hobbies?

Captain: Sure! I love to spend time trainin' my guard roach, Max to attack that runty torch bearer Crumb...heh heh heh.

M.Hess: Oh, OK. WOW, will you look at the time! I guess you need to be getting back to the Queen's Royal Chamber, eh?

Captain: Heh...Yeah I gotta go use the throne...BWAHAHAHAHAAA! (Cough! Wheeze)

M.Hess: Oh, GROSS! Thank you for taking the time, Captain...Um...Sherbet.

Hope you enjoyed the interview, everyone!

BONUS CHARACTER ART

THE OVENLAND CASTLE DESIGN

The first sketch for the Ovenland Castle...
Was a GIANT cast iron potbelly stove. I wanted more room and chambers that Oven Frites could live in so I made it into a tower of petrified grease. Ew!

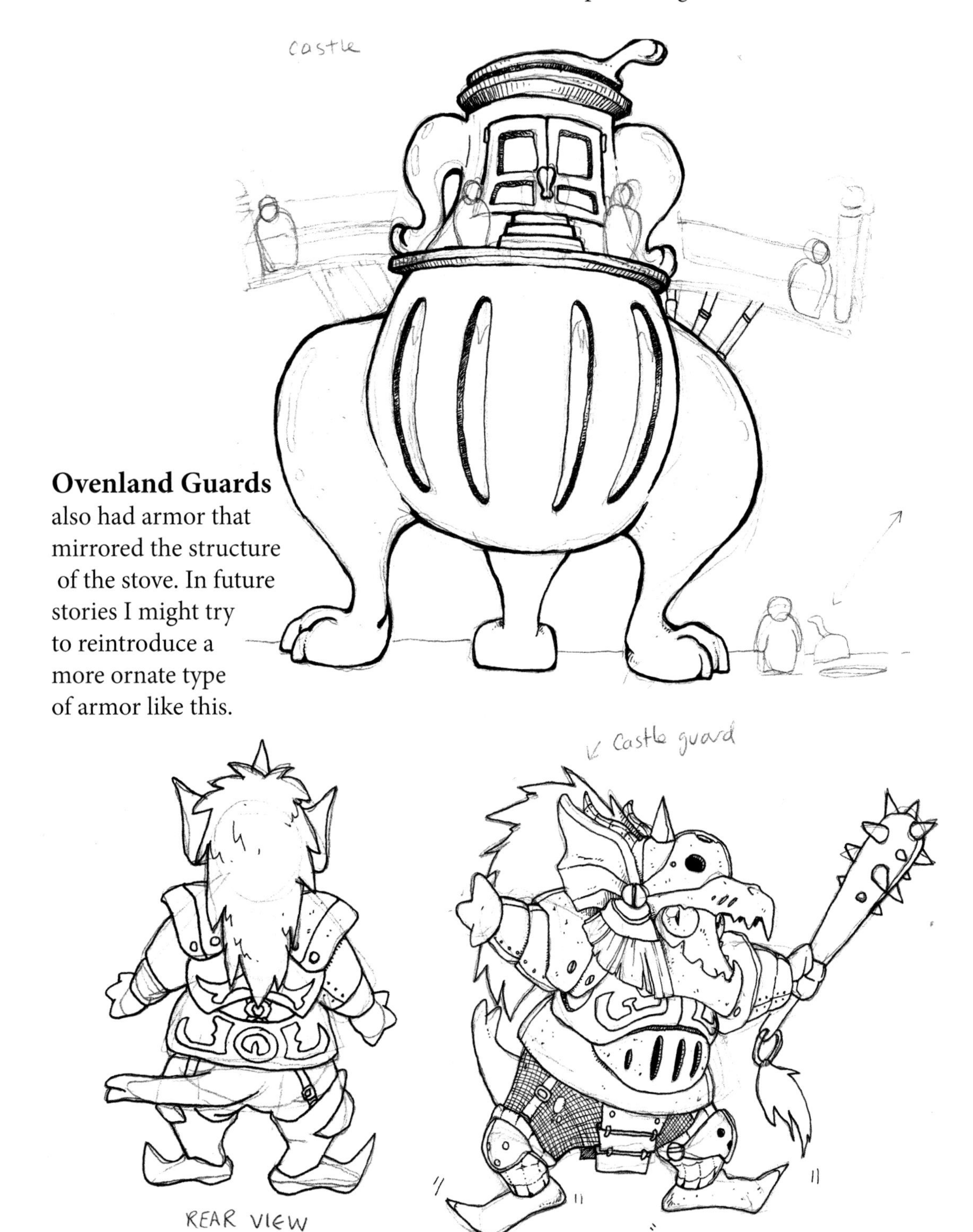

Ovenland Guards also had armor that mirrored the structure of the stove. In future stories I might try to reintroduce a more ornate type of armor like this.

THE QUEEN OF OVENLAND

Her Royal Highness

In the earliest sketches of the Queen, her throne was smaller and a lot less luxurious. Also, I had a frying pan on her head with an egg in it. I liked the idea of having a steaming, bubbling pot on her head that would intensify based on her mood...which is usually angry.

THE ROYAL GUARD OF OVENLAND

For the original Guard Frite uniform
The guards were actually skinnier and had longer, skinnier legs. I wanted these creatures to seem bigger, heavier, and MORE intimidating, so I made the shoulder guards much bigger. I took away the head dress and mask.

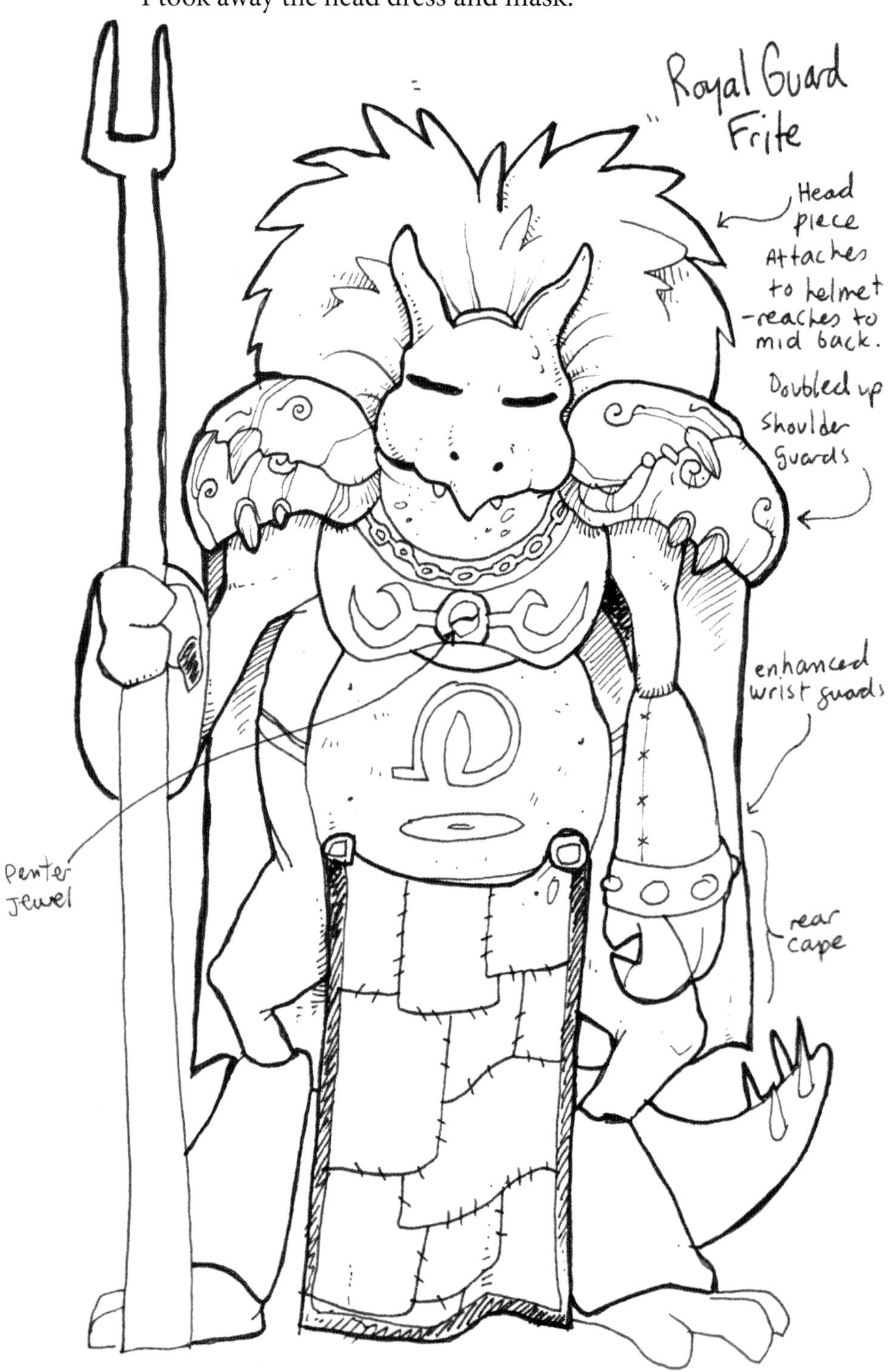

CRUMB: A DRUDGE FROM OVENLAND

Did you know?
Originally, I designed the Oven Frites with long, skinny legs and tails that they could balance on. Later on, I ended up giving them short, stumpy legs to enhance the sense of them being short and low to the ground.

SKETCH OF LILLY BROWN

Early sketch of Lilly Brown

Here is an early sketch that I made of Lilly. Initially, she had a skirt on, but I since changed her to having cargo shorts because I figured that was better suited to oven-based adventuring!

THANKS FOR STOPPING BY!

**I hope you enjoyed reading about Lilly's adventure.
If you'd like to find out more about what's happening with Lilly, read about the various characters, find out the latest news, and get a peek at cool preview art, go to:**

www.facebook.com/ovenland

THE LITTLE BLACK FISH
AN ADAPTATION
OF SAMAD BEHRANGI'S STORY
ART BY BIZHAN KHODABANDEH